## *"You're making fun of me, Jack Madden," Ellin accused.*

"I'd never do that, Ellin Bennett."

His words were spoken as softly as a lover's caress. For a crazy moment, she longed for his touch on her skin, the brush of his full lips against hers. She was mesmerized by a need so intense, it caused a physical ache.

Holy guacamole! What was she thinking? "It's getting late. I need to put Lizzie to bed."

She stood up and leaned over to lift her sleeping daughter from his arms. She heard his sharp intake of breath when her hair swung down and brushed his cheek.

Her eyes met his. For one heart-stopping minute she knew he meant to kiss her. And she was stunned to realize how much she wanted him to....

Dear Reader,

Summer's finally here! Whether you'll be lounging poolside, at the beach, or simply in your home this season, we have great reads packed with everything you enjoy from Silhouette Romance—tenderness, emotion, fun and, of course, heart-pounding romance—plus some very special surprises.

First, don't miss the exciting conclusion to the thrilling ROYALLY WED: THE MISSING HEIR miniseries with Cathie Linz's *A Prince at Last!* Then be swept off your feet—just like the heroine herself!—in Hayley Gardner's *Kidnapping His Bride.*

Romance favorite Raye Morgan is back with *A Little Moonlighting,* about a tycoon set way off track by his beguiling associate who wants a family to call her own. And in Debrah Morris's *That Maddening Man,* can a traffic-stopping smile convince a career woman—and single mom—to slow down…?

Then laugh, cry and fall in love all over again with two incredibly tender love stories. Vivienne Wallington's *Kindergarten Cupids* is a very different, highly emotional story about scandal, survival and second chances. Then dive right into Jackie Braun's *True Love, Inc.,* about a professional matchmaker who's challenged to find her very sexy, very cynical client his perfect woman. Can she convince him that she already has?

Here's to a wonderful, relaxing summer filled with happiness and romance. See you next month with more fun-in-the-sun selections.

Happy reading!

*Mary-Theresa Hussey*

Mary-Theresa Hussey
Senior Editor

Please address questions and book requests to:
Silhouette Reader Service
U.S.: 3010 Walden Ave., P.O. Box 1325, Buffalo, NY 14269
Canadian: P.O. Box 609, Fort Erie, Ont. L2A 5X3

# That Maddening Man

## DEBRAH MORRIS

SILHOUETTE *Romance*

Published by Silhouette Books

America's Publisher of Contemporary Romance

Special thanks to Steve Ferguson of the Texoma Volunteer Fire Department, Lake Texoma, Kingston, Oklahoma, for answering my questions and helping me get the facts right.

And to my wonderful critique partners: Willie, Donnell and Sheila. Thanks for all your help, support and inspiration.

 SILHOUETTE BOOKS

ISBN 0-373-19597-4

THAT MADDENING MAN

Visit Silhouette at www.eHarlequin.com

**Printed in U.S.A.**

**Books by Debrah Morris**

Silhouette Romance

*A Girl, a Guy and a Lullaby* #1549
*That Maddening Man* #1597

---

## DEBRAH MORRIS

Before embarking on a solo writing career, Debrah Morris coauthored over twenty romance novels as one half of the Pepper Adams/Joanna Jordan writing team. She's been married for twenty-four years, and between them, she and her husband have five children. She's changed careers several times in her life, but finds she much prefers writing to working. She loves to hear from readers. Please contact her at P.O. Box 522, Norman, OK 73070-0522. If you would like an autographed bookmark, please send a SASE with your request.

# INTEROFFICE MEMO

TO:     Jack Madden, Roving Reporter

FROM:   Ellin Bennett, Managing Editor of the
        *Washington Post-ette*

RE:     Deadlines

Jack,

I was distressed by the tardiness of your last
article, though a fine piece of journalism. The
intramural boys' soccer teams will be pleased.
When I asked colleagues for the reason for this
tardiness, they replied that you had "taken time
to smell the roses."

Though roses smell fine indeed, this is no way
to run a newspaper. As your boss, I expect you
to adhere to deadlines.


P.S. See you for dinner around six o'clo___

# Chapter One

Ellin Bennett was a risk-taker by nature, but not quite reckless enough to drive these hills at the posted speed limit. Her gloved hands tightened on the wheel as she steered the sleek Japanese import along the narrow two-lane highway. There were moments when daring was the way to go, but this was not one of them.

She passed another Watch For Deer sign. Was it a warning? Or an invitation to enjoy the local wildlife? Should she be wary of big-eyed creatures blundering into her path? Or look out for friendly loiterers in the woods? After eleven years in Chicago, living in the Ozarks would take some getting used to.

"But, Mommy, Santa Claus won't know where to find me."

"Sure he will, Lizzie." Ellin glanced in the rearview mirror and smiled. Strapped into a state-of-the-art booster seat, her four-year-old daughter wore a fuzzy pink coat, a gaudy rhinestone tiara and a worried frown.

"I told you, Mommy. I'm *not* Lizzie today."

"So sorry, Your Highness. I meant *Princess* Lizzie, of course." She atoned for the breach of protocol like a chastened vassal. After all, it was her fourth reminder.

"But *how* will he find me?" the child persisted. "He doesn't know we moved in with Grammy."

"Sure he does, honey. Santa Claus knows everything." Ellin wasn't exactly filled with Christmas spirit this year, but she couldn't let her cynicism spoil her little girl's illusions.

"But Grammy doesn't have a chimbly." Normally sunny and easygoing, Lizzie had developed an alarming number of worries since the move. Most of which involved the coming holiday.

"That won't stop Santa."

"He can't leave presents if there's no chimbly to come down."

"Of course he can," Ellin assured with a sigh. "He's magic."

"When are we getting a Christmas tree?" Lizzie twirled her princess wand absently.

"Soon, baby, soon." Ellin watched the twisting road and the ditch looming close beside it.

"Today?"

"Maybe." The absence of a propped-up conifer in the living room was a big source of preschool anxiety.

"Don't say maybe." Lizzie's little pink lips puckered into a pout. "Say yes."

"We'll see." The phrase was straight out of Lesson One of the Mommy Handbook and usually had the desired pacification effect. But not today.

"Santa won't like it if we don't have a Christmas tree," Lizzie warned with arch authority. "He'll be all mad."

"No, he won't. Santa can't get mad at princesses. The tooth fairy won't allow it." Hearing a slurping sound, Ellin glanced at the useless pile of hair on the seat beside her. Pudgy, her grandmother's aptly named Yorkie-Pomeranian was idly gumming the strap of her leather handbag.

"Give me that." She yanked her Kate Spade original out of harm's way. Wrinkling her nose in distaste, she plucked a clump of fawn-colored fur off the upholstery, hit the window button and flicked it onto the gray winter landscape. Not only was Pudgy missing several important teeth, he was going bald.

Her grandmother actually missed the quivering mass of canine nerves and had requested Pudgy's presence at the nursing home's Christmas party today. If neurotic shedding was any indication, Ida Faye's longtime companion missed her, too. Mrs. Polk, the forward-thinking administrator of Shady Acres Care Center and a vocal proponent of pet therapy, thought the visit might hasten the eighty-year-old's recovery from hip surgery.

"Do you know where the angel is, Mommy? The one with the shiny dress that goes on top of the tree?"

"She's safe in a box in Grammy's garage."

"The twinkle lights, too? And the sparkly snowmen?"

"Yes, dear. They're all safe." Giving up the town house on Lake Michigan had been difficult, but it was especially traumatic for Lizzie. She'd cried when the movers crated their belongings for storage and wouldn't stop until Ellin agreed to haul a box of favorite holiday decorations all the way to Arkansas. Her daughter had Christmas on the brain and was convinced that moving had somehow upset universal order at the North Pole.

"Can I see 'em when we get home?" she asked suspiciously.

"Sure, no problem." Despite her reassuring mommy-face, Ellin wasn't too happy about being uprooted either.

Although temporary, her new job was a good example of an old axiom.

*Be careful what you wish for.*

Journalism dreams born during her stint on the *Whitman Junior High Tattler* had evolved into a do-or-die goal in college. Determined to be a managing editor before age thirty-five, Ellin had sacrificed. Struggled. Run the fast track in sensible two-inch heels and leaped over the limp bodies of the less dedicated. Along the way, she'd slowed down enough to marry, have a baby and get divorced, never taking her eyes off the prize.

She'd advanced quickly. The past six months she'd worked as an assignment editor at a respected Chicago newspaper. Her career had been right on track—until the whole thing derailed onto an unexpected siding. In a rush to make deadline *and* Lizzie's first dance recital, she violated a basic law of journalism. She approved a reporter's story without verifying it. Any first-year journalism student would have known better.

"Mommy, is Rudolph a boy or a girl?"

"I'm sure Rudolph is a girl, princess." Surely, only a female with a superwoman complex would attempt to zip around the world in one night, dragging an overweight elf and a sleigh full of toys.

"What about Olive?"

"Olive?" Ellin's brow furrowed.

"You know. Like in the song. Olive the other reindeer." Lizzie sang it for emphasis. "Is Olive a girl or boy?"

"All the reindeer are girls." Had to be. Poor misguided things thought they could have it all.

Ellin had taken responsibility for her mistake, had even tried to point out the irony of the situation to her superiors. A master nitpicker, for once she'd failed to pick enough nit. But they had not been amused. After the public stoning of the overzealous reporter, she'd been called up on the slate-gray Berber and stripped of her parking pass and card key like a court-martialed soldier. Slinking out of the city room in professional disgrace, her first thought was to change her name and move to a third world country.

"Mommy, why doesn't Mrs. Claus help give out the toys?"

"She doesn't like to steal Santa's thunder." Or she was smart enough to stay home with a cup of hot tea while her old man froze his tail off buzzing around the stratosphere.

She had to stop being so cynical. After all, she'd stepped in a colossal pile of doo-doo and had come out smelling like a nosegay, hadn't she? Her career had taken a hit, but her life-long dream was coming true. For the next three months she would be acting editor of the Washington *Post*. And it was still several weeks before her thirty-fifth birthday.

Problem was, it wasn't *The Washington Post,* the grand-daddy of all newspapers. Nor was her new home in the nation's fast-paced capital. It was in Washington, Arkansas, where life moved at the speed of a stroked-out snail. The *Washington Post-Ette* was a dinky little weekly with a circulation of less than eight thousand that boasted of keeping its fourth estate finger firmly on the pulse of the chicken-raising industry.

According to the owner, its original name was the *Post-Gazette,* but the "Gaz" had been dropped at some point in its illustrious history. The shortened form was better suited to a toaster snack than to a hard-hitting shaper of public opinion.

For the time being, she could pretty much forget about a Pulitzer.

"Is Christmas really Jesus' birthday?" Lizzie asked.

"Yes, dear. At least that's when we celebrate it."

"So why do *I* get presents?" Her small forehead wrinkled in confusion. "It's not *my* birthday."

"Remember? It's one of those tradition things I told you about." Vague perhaps, but the experts advised against giving children more information than they could handle.

"Oh, yeah." Keeping the beat with her beribboned princess wand, Lizzie hummed an odd mix of "Jingle Bells" and "Mary Had a Little Lamb."

Pudgy wheezed. Ellin glanced down in alarm, concerned that he might have begun the bucket-kicking process on her watch.

"Mommy! Stop! Stop!" Lizzie shrieked. "It's Santa."

Ellin looked back at the road, and her eyes widened in surprise. "Well, I'll be a partridge in a pear tree."

It *was* Santa. Or his body double. Decked out in full St. Nicholas regalia and looking like a Yuletide figment of her little girl's imagination.

"Stop, Mommy! Santa needs help!" Lizzie was squirming and swinging her wand and issuing directives, all at once. Pudgy had recovered from his coughing fit and bounced up and down on the seat, adding his yip-yappy opinion to the excitement.

Stop? For some guy waving his arms in the middle of the road? No way. Ellin was a city girl and stuck to a strict "No Hitchhikers" policy. She didn't brake for strangers, not even the jolly old elf himself.

"I don't think so, princess." She wouldn't stop, but she didn't want to run the guy down. She slowed to give him a chance to get his velvet-covered butt out of the road and noticed a shiny crimson pickup truck angled off the shoulder.

"Maybe Santa needs our help because Rudolph got hurt." In view of the Watch For Deer signs, Lizzie's explanation had a certain preschool logic. "Or maybe the sleigh broke down. Stop, Mommy, stop!"

She had to. He gave no indication of moving out of the way. Suspicious, Ellin punched the door locks and lowered the window an inch. Hmm. Given his elfin-based gene structure, Santa was much taller than one might expect. He stepped up to the car and smiled. At least she thought he smiled. It was hard to tell exactly what was going on under that curling white beard.

"I'm sorry to trouble you, ma'am." His drawl was soft and articulate, a little too down-south for an inhabitant of the polar regions. "But I wonder if you might have a cell phone I could use?"

"No, I don't." Then she realized how vulnerable her admission made her. "But I have a black belt in karate and an attack dog trained to kill on command." Pudgy's yip would pierce armor-plated eardrums. "Drowning in dog slobber is an unpleasant way to go."

He might have smiled again as he peered in at the toy-sized dog. "Thanks for the warning. I ran out of gas. I've been meaning to get the gas gauge fixed, but I put it off a little too long." He shrugged and grinned. Quite disarmingly. "Looks like I'm stuck."

"Sorry. I don't have any gas, either."

"Where's your sleigh, Santa?" Born verbal, Lizzie had no qualms about jumping into adult conversation.

"Can't drive the sleigh without snow, darlin.' I had to use the truck today."

"Does it fly?"

"Nope. That's why I need gas." He turned to Ellin. "I'm running behind schedule. I'm due at Shady Acres in a few minutes. Big Christmas party for the residents. The old folks are really looking forward to it, and I'd hate to disappoint them. It's just up the road. Could you give me a lift?''

Not hardly. A deserted road. Stranger. Unarmed female with small child and wheezy dog. It had all the makings of a late-breaking news story. But, she reminded herself, this was not Chicago. Washington, Arkansas, wasn't exactly a teeming hotbed of criminal activity. Besides, would the roadside strangler go to the trouble of donning a beautifully made, fur-trimmed, ruby-red crushed velvet Santa suit, complete with shiny black knee boots, wide silver-buckle and jaunty cap?

She thought not.

''Mommy!''

Ellin looked back at Lizzie and wondered if the callous treatment of a childhood icon might someday propel her daughter into therapy. ''What, honey?''

''Give Santa a ride so I can tell him where my new house is.''

Like she'd let that happen. ''Actually, I'm headed for Shady Acres myself,'' she told the man behind the fake beard and pillow-stuffed tummy. He wore wire-rimmed glasses, a shoulder-length white wig that curled on un-elfishly wide shoulders and a big, droopy mustache that twitched when he smiled.

She lowered the window another inch. ''I'll give you a ride. *If* you can tell me the administrator's name.''

''Is this some kind of test?''

He might not be Santa, but his brown eyes definitely twinkled. ''Not as in ACT, but I need proof you're telling the truth.''

''Mommy! Santa Claus wouldn't fib.'' Lizzie was scandalized.

The man in the Santa suit laughed. The rich sound was

like aged brandy, and made Ellin feel flushed and warm all over. "I need to be careful."

"I appreciate your caution. The administrator's name is Lorella Polk. She's fifty-eight years old. Married to Henry Polk, mother of Bobby, Tracy and Paul. She has four grandchildren. Allen, Lindsey, Derrick and Ty. She belongs to the First Baptist Church and sings alto in the choir. She's been running the nursing home for twelve years. Before that, she had a home decor party business and before that, she sold cosmetics door-to-door. She had her gall bladder removed last year and has to watch her cholesterol. Recently, she developed an annoying rash on her—"

"That'll do," Ellin said briskly. "What are you? The local operative for the North Pole CIA?"

He leaned down and smiled through the window at Lizzie. "Santa Claus knows everything. Right, princess?"

Lizzie beamed and waved her wand, clearly gratified to meet someone who recognized royalty when he saw it.

"Right." With a sigh, Ellin unlocked the door. Father Christmas fetched a big canvas bag full of brightly wrapped presents from his truck and placed it in the back seat. Then he slid in beside her and Pudgy, and arranged his long legs.

Wow, she thought as she accelerated. Who would have guessed a guy who hung out with reindeer would smell so nice?

"Do you gots a surprise for me in your sack, Santa?" Lizzie asked hopefully.

He turned and gave the little girl a solemn look. "I just might. But you'll have to wait until the party to find out."

"Goody! Mommy says you don't need a chimbly to get into my house on Christmas Eve. Is that true?" Apparently, even four-year-olds knew to verify questionable data.

"Your mommy's right about that."

"Let me hear you go ho, ho, ho," the princess commanded.

"Okay." He gathered a deep, dramatic breath, clamped both hands on his sizable tummy, and let loose a rumbling trio of hos.

Ellin frowned, then smiled at her daughter's obvious delight. Who *was* this man?

"Hey, Pudgy, how ya doin' old buddy?" He ruffled the dog's fur, and the beast crawled into his ample lap.

"How do you know my grandmother's dog?"

"Santa knows everything, Mommy." The princess had long since perfected a tone of superiority when dealing with her subjects. "He sees you when you're sleeping. He knows when you're awake."

The man didn't miss a beat. "He knows when you've been bad or good," he sang in an ingenuous baritone that rumbled through the car's interior.

"So be good for good'ess sake." Lizzie finished with a reprimanding shake of her tiny finger. At least all the hours they'd spent on the trip listening to the same two Christmas CDs over and over had paid off.

"I probably don't need to tell you this," Ellin said with a sidelong glance at her mysterious passenger. "But my name is Ellin Bennett and that's Princess Lizzie."

He patted the dog with his white-gloved hand. "I know who you are. I'm—"

"Santa Claus, of course." Ellin cocked her head in Lizzie's direction, warning him with a look not to destroy the little girl's illusions.

"That's right. Santa Claus. Ho, ho, ho."

Jack Madden knew exactly who Ellin Bennett was, but the dark-eyed brunette was not the hard-driving piranha he'd expected. He'd heard all about the big city journalist in town to take over the paper while Jig Baker was in Peru living his dream of participating in a full-scale university-sponsored archaeological dig.

Jig had said she was a career-minded divorcée with a young daughter. He warned Jack she was used to doing things differently in Chicago and might make some changes during her tenure. So be prepared.

But nothing could have prepared him for these two. Even Mrs. Boswell had failed to mention that the granddaughter she'd recommended for the job was a striking beauty. She'd bragged about her great-granddaughter, but never said she was such a precocious little angel.

Jack moonlighted as the paper's sports editor and roving reporter, so he was curious about the new boss. He satisfied that curiosity by watching her openly as she maneuvered the winding road. Word around town, she was a hard-nosed newspaperwoman. But from where he sat, her nose looked anything but hard.

In fact, everything about the big city hotshot looked enticingly soft. Touch-me-and-see-for-yourself-soft. She had peachy pale skin and thick-lashed golden brown eyes. Full lips the color of his mother's coral tea roses. Her long brown hair was twisted into a gravity-defying arrangement skewered by two ebony chopsticks.

Jack was thrown off balance by the sudden urge to reach over and slip out those silly sticks, just to watch the whiskey-colored mass tumble down. He managed to resist temptation but had an unbidden image of classy Ellin Bennett wearing her little girl's endearingly fake tiara. And nothing else.

The Santa suit suddenly became too warm for comfort. A master of restraint, he didn't usually have such inappropriate thoughts about a woman he'd just met. But this one was having a profound effect on him…a very pleasant effect.

He couldn't take his gaze off her. She looked more like a delicate old-fashioned cameo than the competitive work-aholic Jig had described. Maybe the softness was part of her ensemble, to be shrugged on and off as occasion de-manded. Like the creamy angora turtleneck and brown woolen slacks, the camel coat and expensive boots. He noted the delicate gold watch on her wrist and the little diamond studs in her earlobes. Tasteful, understated. And utterly feminine.

Jack smiled. They were definitely in for some changes. Watching this urbane beauty adapt to small-town living might very well be the most entertaining thing to happen in Washington for years. The thought of getting to know her better filled him with a sense of anticipation he hadn't felt since he was a kid waiting for Christmas himself.

"So, how's Ida Faye doing?" Ellin's feisty old grand-mother was one of his favorite people. He'd visited her several times since her discharge from the hospital and knew she wasn't happy being "incarcerated" in the nursing home. His Aunt Lorella made sure she received the best of care.

"You know my grandmother?" Ellin's puzzled look was replaced by a smug knowing one. "Oh, I'm sorry, I forgot. Santa knows—"

"Everything!" Jack and Lizzie called out in unison.

"Right." Ellin flipped on the turn signal and pulled into the nursing home drive.

"I warned her not to shovel snow at her age." Jack hoped he would be as spry as Mrs. Boswell in his eightieth winter. "But you know Ida. Always helping everyone."

Ellin parked near the door and switched off the engine. "Well, this time she helped herself to a broken hip and a doctor-ordered stay at Shady Acres."

She dropped the car keys in her coat pocket, opened the

back door, unsnapped the child restraint and lifted the little girl out. Pudgy bounced around their feet.

Jack hoisted the big sack of presents over his shoulder in true Santa style. He looked down when he felt a small mittened hand clutch his fingers. Lizzie held on tightly, her mouth curved in an impish grin, the phony crown askew atop her long blond curls. Those blue eyes could melt the frostiest snowman's heart.

Jack squeezed her hand. Reaching into his pack, he produced a large brass schoolhouse bell and knelt to her level. "Can you help me, Lizzie?"

"You need *my* help?" she asked, surprised.

"Yes, I do. Can you ring this special bell to let everyone know Santa Claus is coming?"

Her face lit up at the prospect. "I sure can."

Holding the bell reverently in one small hand, she clutched his fingers with the other. Jack suspected this would be a day little Lizzie Bennett would remember forever.

Maybe he would, too.

Together, they walked up the sidewalk to Shady Acres Care Center. Ellin held the door open by leaning against it, her arms folded across her chest.

He winked at her as he passed, enjoying her startled response. But she played it cool. Clearly not a woman who backed down from a challenge, she didn't blush or glance away or look flustered. He liked the idea that she would give as good as she got. Staring boldly back at him, she wore the bemused expression of a smart, savvy woman who has been there, done everything, but had finally encountered something she simply could not understand.

Jack Madden had never been so intrigued.

# *Chapter Two*

Ellin and Lizzie entered the winter-bright dayroom ahead of Santa, whose arrival was heralded by the little girl's enthusiastic bell-ringing. A fragrant Douglas fir in the corner was as laden with ornaments, tinsel and lights as the red-draped refreshment table was with treats. Elderly residents wearing holly corsages and expectant expressions sat in easy chairs and wheelchairs arranged in a circle around the perimeter.

Ellin smiled and waved when she spotted her grandmother. Ida Faye sat in a wheelchair on the far side of the room, her knobby, arthritic hands clutched in her lap. She had a red scarf around her neck and a colorful afghan over her legs. Her thin white hair was carefully parted, held in place by plastic barrettes like Lizzie's.

Ellin was struck anew by how small and frail she'd become since the accident. Celebrating her eightieth Christmas this year, she wouldn't have many more. Due to her parents' divorce, Ellin hadn't spent much time with her paternal grandmother over the years and hoped it wasn't too late to make up for lost time. It was important for Lizzie to know her great-grandmother, to feel connected to her family. But it might never have happened if circumstances had been different.

Ellin worried that by leaving Chicago she'd taken the coward's way out. That coming to this remote little town meant she was running away from her problems instead of solving them. But then she saw how Ida Faye's face lit up when they walked in, and she knew there were things more important than her career. What had seemed like a fall from grace now seemed more like a blessing in disguise. Only a fool would turn down a sudden, if undeserved, gift of fate.

She and Lizzie lavished Ida Faye with big hugs and damp kisses. Then Ellin deposited Pudgy in his mistress's lap. He stood on his hind legs to lick her pale, wrinkled cheek.

"I'm so glad ya'll could come. And thank you for bringing this old rascal to see me. I've missed him so."

"He's missed you, too." Ellin helped Lizzie out of her coat and mittens, noting the smiles her outfit generated.

When it came to fashion statements, her only child believed individuality was the way to go. Today she'd insisted on wearing her pink ballet slippers and a puffy-sleeved, full-length princess dress constructed of frilled layers of pink and purple chiffon. According to Lizzie, it wasn't just a Halloween costume. It was appropriate party attire.

"Okay now, that's enough, Pudge." Ida Faye settled the dog down for a petting session. Then she gave Ellin a wide, denture-baring grin. She whispered behind her hand so Lizzie wouldn't hear. "Ain't that Jack a honey?"

"Who?" Someone brought a chair and Ellin scooted it close. Lizzie settled on the floor at her feet, Santa's bell in her lap.

"Jack Madden," Ida Faye said. "The young fella playin'

Santy Claus. You oughta know him, you came in with him."

"Oh, so that's his name." It sounded familiar. Where had she heard it before? Ah, yes. The owner of the newspaper had mentioned him. "He works for the paper, right?"

Ida Faye nodded. "Yep. But that's just a sideline. His main profession is schoolteaching. He's good as gold, our Jack is."

"Hmm." Ellin settled back and watched the ersatz Santa work the room while an old lady in a bright red dress pounded "Here Comes Santa Claus" from an out-of-tune piano.

He belted out several rounds of hearty ho, ho, hos, clasping his king-size belly until it shook like the proverbial bowl full of jelly. Then he swung his heavy sack to the floor and strode around the dayroom, greeting the old folks by name and inquiring if they'd been good boys and girls. He shook their blue-veined hands, kissed their blushing cheeks and wiped their sentimental tears.

Then he passed out the gifts Ida Faye said he'd inspired his high school students to collect and wrap. Volunteers and family members helped the elderly residents open them to find the warm socks, slippers, stuffed animals, colorful posters, and bottles of lotion and aftershave inside. Then they passed out sweets and diabetic treats along with cups of holiday punch.

Lizzie tugged on Ellin's slacks. "What is it, honey?"

Her little face scrunched up. "I didn't get a present."

"That's okay. We're just guests at this party."

"But Santa said."

"I know, but—"

"Hey, princess. Did you think I'd forgotten about you?" Santa Claus, alias Jack Madden, handed Lizzie a small bundle wrapped in red tissue paper.

"Oh, no," she denied. "I knew you would never forget *me*. I'm your helper, right?"

"You sure are. Aren't you going to open your present?"

She eagerly ripped off the paper to find a floppy dog with droopy ears and large button eyes. "Oh, my very own puppy," she squealed.

"Do you like him?" Jack asked.

She hugged the toy to her chest. "I *love* him. I've been needing a doggie just like this."

Ellin shook her head. Yeah, right. Lizzie's stuffed animal collection easily filled three or four packing boxes.

"I'm glad to hear that. See that nice lady over there?" Jack pointed discreetly to a sad-looking old woman perched alone on a vinyl-coated sofa.

"Yeah."

"Doesn't she look like she needs to see your doggie? I bet it would make her smile if you went over there and showed it to her."

"Okay." Eager to do Santa's bidding, Lizzie scampered off. Sure enough, the woman's expression was transformed from sadness to delight at the sight of the little girl in the froufrou dress and tiara. Lizzie smiled shyly as a trembling hand reached out to caress her golden curls.

"That was quite a performance, Mr. Madden," Ellin said with a grudging smile. "You make an entirely credible Santa Claus."

"Thank you, Ms. Bennett." A well-brought-up Southern gentleman, he turned solicitously to his elder. "You're looking lovely today, Mrs. Boswell. And how are you feeling?"

"As right as an eighty-year-old cripple with a pin in her hip can feel, I reckon. Jack, I want you to tell that aunt of yours to make them nurses let me stay up and watch *Jeopardy*. They put a body to bed way too early around here."

He patted her hand. "I'll talk to Aunt Lorella and see what I can do."

Ellin looked at him sharply. *Aunt* Lorella? No wonder he'd known the administrator's life story. "So Mrs. Polk is related to you, is she, Mr. Madden?"

His eyes glinted with what would have been called mischief in a ten-year-old. "My mother's sister. But please, call me Jack. After all, we're going to be working together."

"So I hear. What is it exactly you do at the paper?" Ellin had not survived in a difficult profession by being indecisive. She trusted her instincts, made snap judgments and found her first impressions were usually right on target.

But this time she was baffled. She couldn't quite put the Jack Madden puzzle together.

He shrugged. "Whatever needs doing. Jig calls me the sports editor, but the title's just an excuse to attend all the high school football and basketball games in the area."

"I understand you're a teacher."

"Yes, ma'am. High school English."

"I want to thank you for being so nice to Lizzie today. The move was hard on her. Meeting you, I mean Santa Claus, really made her day."

"I was happy to do it," he said with a shrug. "She's a real cutie pie."

"Thanks for playing along with her fantasies. I hope you don't mind staying in character a bit longer. She isn't up to speed on St. Nick mythology."

"Not a problem," he told her. "If you ladies will excuse me, I need to call a friend to come and haul me to a gas station so I can retrieve my truck and go home." He turned to walk away.

"Mr. Madden? Wait." It was out of character for Ellin

to extend herself in such a way. Normally, she managed her problems and expected others to do the same.

But thoughts of fate and its unexpected gifts lingered in her mind. Combined with her under-exercised conscience it tweaked her into action. Here was a chance to help a man who'd gone out of his way to be nice to her daughter, her grandmother and a whole crowd of old people.

"You can call me Jack when Lizzie's not around," he said.

She tried to ignore his comment, but that sexy, Rhett Butler accent did some tweaking of its own. "I'll drive you to the gas station." It wasn't so much an offer as it was a revelation of fact. Once Ellin made up her mind to do something, it was a done deal. "Then I'll take you to your truck."

"That's very generous, but I wouldn't want to put you out in any way."

His tone of voice, along with the look in his eyes, let her know that he was well aware of being bossed around. Apparently, it amused him.

"Nonsense. I said I'd drive you. So I'll drive." Her words were a bit crisper around the edges than she intended.

"Well, if you're sure."

The man had to have the most intriguing eyes Ellin had ever seen. Because the rest of his face was concealed beneath the curly white beard, her attention focused on the intelligence and humor sparking behind those wire-rims. Something in their depths made her want to know him better.

And figure out just what made him tick.

It might be interesting to discover this paragon's faults. Surely, the guy had some of those. "Just let me know when you're ready to go." She used her best managerial voice.

"Okay, then." His gaze swept the room, lighting on several residents who appeared to need a bit more cheer. "I want to mingle a little longer. How's half an hour sound?"

"Fine."

"Don't forget to talk to Lorella," Ida Faye called after him as he walked away.

The old woman smiled and reached out to squeeze Ellin's hand. "You're in Arkansas now, Ellie."

"I know that." She was still wondering what had possessed her to offer to help Jack Madden. Ordinarily, it would never have crossed her mind to reach out like that. But given the lengths he was willing to go to, just to bring a little happiness to others, it would have taken a harder heart than hers to refuse the call.

"Well, seems to me, you're still acting like Chicago." Her grandmother gave her a knowing look.

"What do you mean?"

"Around here, honey, folks are more friendly-like than maybe you're used to in the city."

"I was friendly," she protested. "I said I'd help him."

"It weren't *what* you said, Ellie." Ida Faye cackled. "It were the way you said it."


Jack made good on his promise and remained firmly in Santa mode. After seeing Ida Faye back to her room and helping her into bed for a nap, Ellin drove him to the nearest station where he borrowed a gas can and filled it at the pump. Several people spoke to him in the process, calling him by name. She was amazed so many seemed to recognize him beneath the disguise. Granted, Washington wasn't that big, but he couldn't know everyone in town, could he? She hadn't even met the people who lived next door to her in Chicago.

Excited by the party and fueled by high-octane sugar

cookies and candy canes, Lizzie monopolized the conversation on the drive back to the stranded truck.

"We don't gots a Christmas tree yet, Santa." The can-you-believe-the-injustice-of-that was implied in her tone.

"What with the move and all, we haven't had time to buy one yet," Ellin said defensively. How could she admit to a man in a red velvet suit that she couldn't muster enough holiday spirit to provide her child the most basic of Christmas traditions?

"You don't buy Christmas trees around here," Jack scoffed.

"You don't? Where do you get 'em then?" Lizzie was always willing to learn something new.

"Why, you go out to the woods and chop one down. Don't tell me you've never chopped down your own Christmas tree?" he asked with mock disbelief.

Lizzie shook her head solemnly. "Nope. Can you help us chop a tree, Santa?"

"Well, I have to get back to the North Pole and make sure those elves make enough toys for the children." Her little face fell, so he added, "But I have a special friend named Jack who would be happy to take you and your mommy out to the woods."

"I just bet he would," Ellin muttered. What was he thinking? Didn't he know how dangerous it was to plant an idea like that in the fertile imagination of a four-year-old?

"Can we, Mommy? I never been to Christmas tree woods before. Oh, no! We don't have somethin' to chop with."

"My buddy Jack has an ax." He smiled at Ellin. "A big one."

Ellin raised one brow. "Oh? He should be careful. A guy who doesn't know what he's doing could get hurt."

Santa Jack winced. ''I'll warn him.''

''Can we go today?'' Lizzie was all atwitter at the prospect of not only chopping down a tree, but meeting one of Santa's special friends.

''That's up to your mother.'' Jack shot Ellin a look that was pure challenge.

''Can we, Mommy? Plee-e-se?''

Ellin decided Jack Madden knew exactly what he was doing. He'd set her up to score major villain points if she vetoed the plan now.

''Maybe.''

Lizzie pushed out her bottom lip and folded her arms on the padded restraint. ''You say maybe, but that just means no.''

''It does not.'' Ellin didn't like being put in the hot seat. She was used to getting what she wanted and it wasn't often someone turned the tables on her. Jack Madden might be good as gold, but he was also sly as a fox.

''Say yes!'' Lizzie whacked the back of Ellin's seat with her wand, either to get her attention or magically change her mind.

''Okay!'' Wow. She'd just been suckered by Santa Claus. She eased on the brakes when she spotted Jack's truck.

Lizzie went from pouty to perky in ten seconds flat. ''We're gonna chop a Christmas tree.''

Santa grinned. ''I'll tell my old buddy Jack to swing by your place later this afternoon. Around four o'clock?''

Ellin shoved the gearshift into Park with more force than was needed and popped open the trunk. ''Fine. We're staying at Ida Faye's.''

''Oh, he knows where you live.'' He sounded like a character in a cheesy horror movie. ''Dress warmly. It gets cold out in the woods.''

Ellin answered his gotcha grin with a frosty glare. He shivered. "Oooh. It's getting a little chilly in *here*. He turned to Lizzie. "You stay good, princess."

"I will," she promised. "Tell your friend Jack to help us chop down a *big* tree."

'I'll do it. Will you put out some cookies before you go to bed on Christmas Eve?"

"Yep. You like chocat chip? Or peanut butter?"

He appeared to think it over. "Chocolate chip, I think." He gave Ellin a smart little salute as he got out to retrieve the gas can. "You have yourself a merry little Christmas, Ms. Bennett."

"Yeah, yeah. You, too." What an exasperating man. She'd like to deck Kriss Kringle's halls for him.

"So, what's she like?" Jana McGovern folded her arms on her desk and leaned forward in the classic pose of one who is all ears.

"She's nice enough." After changing out of the Santa suit, Jack had stopped by his twin sister's small accounting office to get permission to cut a tree on the wooded property she owned with her husband Ted. As usual, he could not escape her evil clutches without first being grilled like a slab of sirloin.

"You sure about that? Because I heard she was a real pain in the butt." Jana poured two cups of coffee and set one in front of her brother. "I believe 'stuck up' was the sobriquet of choice."

"I think she's just—"

"Aloof?" Jana supplied helpfully. "Arrogant?"

"I was going to say self-assured and outspoken."

"You're too nice, little brother," she dismissed. "Poor Jig had to kick his blood pressure medicine up a notch after one brief meeting with the lady in question. Owen wouldn't come out of the men's room for an hour.''

Jack smiled. Owen Larsen, the newspaper's layout artist and town's oldest bachelor, was notoriously shy. "She's not so bad.''

"Looking?''

"What?''

"Is she as attractive as I've heard?''

"Depends on what you call attractive.'' Jack couldn't afford to give her any encouragement. Minding her own business was not a life skill Jana had mastered.

She was always after him, nipping at his heels like a determined cattle dog. According to her, he'd needed to get back out in the world, take another chance, have another adventure. Use his God-given writing talent, and most importantly, fall in love. Apparently, being older by seven minutes entitled her to tell him what to do.

She just didn't get it. He liked waking up every morning knowing exactly what the day would bring. Predictability was highly underrated, in his opinion. He knew all too well what the rest of the world had to offer and liked this part of it better. She accused him of being an underachiever, but he was just an old-fashioned guy trying to make a difference right where he was. He enjoyed both his jobs. He couldn't imagine leaving his many friends to live among strangers.

And adventures? They were more often misadventures with ugly consequences.

"Attractive may be a subjective term,'' Jana said. "But most of us agree on its basic meaning. So how good-looking is she?''

"Somewhere between mud fence and Mona Lisa.''

She gave him a knowing look. "Oh! You like her. I can tell.''

"You can't *tell* anything."

"Hah! Of course, I can. You're not talking about her, so therefore, you think she's hot."

"Remind me again," he drawled. "Is it Aristotelian or Ramistic logic that enables you to reach such truly cockamamie conclusions?"

"Jack, you little devil." Jana reached out and patted his cheek. "You're spouting big words. You are definitely working on a serious crush here."

He gave her a concerned look. "Will you be visiting our planet much longer? Or do you plan to catch the mothership next time it's in town?"

"Hey, there's nothing wrong with you getting a little action, for a change."

"For your information, twisted sister, I happen to get plenty of action." He dated. Some. He was waiting for the right woman to come along. The woman his father assured him he would "know" when he met her. The one who'd "turn him inside out and five ways to Sunday." He wanted happily ever after and the kind of relationship his parents had. Up until today, he hadn't met anyone who even remotely filled the bill.

Jana laughed. "Sure you do. Like I get plenty of chances to dance on MTV. Just be careful, little brother. She's older than you, *and* she's from the big wicked city. A woman like Ellin Bennett will chew you up and spit you out like an Arkansas hairball."

Jack rolled his eyes. "What colorful imagery, Jana. Maybe you should be a writer."

"Nah, I'll leave it to you. So how's the book coming?"

"On its own terms." Jack had long since stopped trying to explain right-brained activities to his left-brained sister. "Writing isn't like bookkeeping."

"When was the last time you worked on it?" she demanded.

"What are you, my conscience?" He finished his coffee. "I didn't come in here to be pecked to death. You don't understand the creative process."

She snorted in derision. "What do you mean? I'm creative."

"You're an accountant," he reminded dryly. "Being creative could land you in the slammer. Now, are you going to let me cut the damn tree or not?"

She fished the key to the property gate out of her purse with a big grin. "Here you go, Don Hemingway Juan. Knock yourself out."

Ellin was poking Lizzie's arms and legs into her purple snowsuit when someone knocked on the door. She glanced at Ida Faye's weird clock that burst into birdsong every hour, on the hour. Madden was right on time.

"Just a minute!" She zipped Lizzie up and tucked her hair into her stocking cap. "There. Run and open the door for Santa's friend."

She collected her parka and purse. She had changed into a heavy sweater, jeans and thick-soled boots. She snugged a wide knit headband over her ears and dashed into the living room.

If she had been one of Lizzie's Saturday morning cartoon characters, the rug would have accordioned as she plowed to a stop and her eyes would have popped out on springs. The man standing by the door, his hands clasped behind his back, could not be Santa Jack.

He was younger than she'd expected. Way younger. A good four or five years her junior, for sure. And taller than she remembered. Without the extra pillow padding, his slim, well-built physique was even more impressive. Wide shoulders. Trim waist. Narrow hips. And, unless she was completely out of touch with reality, which was possible considering she'd agreed to this rendezvous, that heavy seaman's coat concealed a nicely developed chest and biceps.

His brown hair was cut in a short, messy-trendy style that he must have combed with his hand. With his eyes closed. His bottom lip was fuller than the top and high cheekbones lent his face an interesting angularity. The arching brows were brown, not white. And without the beard, well, you really had to admire the strong chin.

He wasn't soap-opera handsome. His features weren't quite perfect enough. But damn, he was cute. Adorable. Like a great big, cuddly, overgrown elf. He still wore the wire-rims, which were obviously not part of the costume, and the smug look in the merry eyes behind the lenses indicated just how much he was enjoying her discomfort. He opened the door with a lopsided grin and dramatic flourish.

"Mommy, this is Santa's friend Jack." Lizzie performed the necessary introductions as they walked to the street. "And guess what? He gots a truck just like Santa's."

"What a coincidence."

He grinned. "So. Ellin Bennett. How're you this fine day?"

It took her a moment to respond. Jack Madden was just full of surprises. "Fine."

"Are you ladies ready to chop down a Christmas tree?" He opened the truck door, and she and Lizzie climbed inside.

"Yeah!" Lizzie submitted to being buckled into a regular lap belt on the seat between them but couldn't sit still.

Ellin pulled on her gloves as though her composure were perfectly intact. Jack gallantly ignored her as he drove out of town. By directing his comments to Lizzie, he gave her time to get over her initial shock.

What had happened to her internal alarm? It was supposed to warn her when she was about to do something really stupid, but it seemed to be malfunctioning today. She considered bailing out and running back to the house. She didn't trust that instant spark of attraction that had cranked up her heart rate and interfered with her objectivity. She knew how dangerous desire could be.

Something was happening here, chemistry-wise. It might feel good, but it was bad. It was beyond bad. The man aroused feelings she'd hadn't felt in a long time. They would only complicate things, and her life was plenty complicated enough. If she were to research "Bad Idea" on the Internet, Jack Madden's name would definitely pop up.

Then she looked at Lizzie's excited little face. How could she deny her only child a much-anticipated experience?

It wasn't like this was a date, she told herself. It didn't have to be the start of anything. In fact, she was probably reading far more into it than she should. The man was just being neighborly. Wasn't that what people did in Arkansas? What was she so worried about? They would get the stupid Christmas tree to make Lizzie happy, and that would be the end of it. It was up to her to keep their relationship strictly professional. She could do that. She wasn't known as the Ice Queen of Chicago for nothing.

So what was the problem?

Him. Her. The situation. Spending time alone in the woods with a charmer who didn't even know how appealing he was. Letting herself get close to someone she'd have to leave behind in a few months. The list could go on and on, but the point was Jack Madden would be nothing but trouble. And it was her policy to not go out looking for trouble. It found her often enough on its own.

Jack looked at her over Lizzie's head, and his grin sent a rush of heat through her. Why did she feel he could actually read her thoughts? This was not good. As Ida Faye would put it, she was poking a wildcat with a short stick.

## Chapter Three

While Jack steered the truck in and out of winding hairpin curves with practiced ease, Ellin fielded Lizzie's questions and faked intense interest in the country landscape. Having spent her entire life within city limits, she was not accustomed to seeing nature as it was in northwestern Arkansas. Trees and gnarled underbrush flourished with in-your-face abandon just beyond the reach of highway brush-cutting crews.

Brown and russet leaves carpeted the ground beneath winter-bare trees. Oaks, hickories and bois d'arcs stretched gray limbs toward the pale, cloudless sky. Tall pines and squat cedars splashed the drab hillsides with waves of green.

Across the valley, the land rolled to the horizon in a crazy quilt of muted colors. Here and there, wispy columns of smoke spiraled from chimneys and flues and drifted lazily above the treetops.

"How much longer?" Lizzie bounced on the seat, unable to contain her excitement.

"Nearly there." Jack flipped on the turn signal and angled off the highway onto a rocky track that wound through the trees. When they came to a heavy gate secured with a looped chain, he stopped, set the brake, and jumped out to release the padlock. The gate swung wide.

"Holy-moley! Is this a road?" Ellin asked skeptically as the truck began its bone-jarring climb up the hill.

"Actually it's an old dry stream bed." He explained the property belonged to his sister and brother-in-law who'd given him permission to cut a tree from an upland meadow. "They had the bed leveled to make it easier to get in and out."

"You call this level?" Ellin braced her hand against the dash. "And easier?"

"For these parts, it is." Jack drove carefully. He didn't want to blow a tire or knock the front wheels out of alignment. "Jana and Ted drive SUVs," he said. "They don't have any trouble getting up to Crazy Bear Holler."

"Crazy Bear Holler?" Lizzie giggled. "That's a silly name."

"It is, isn't it?" Jack grinned down at the little girl. "But back in the 1800s a mean old bear terrorized the homesteads around here. The men tried tracking it down with dogs, but they couldn't find his trail."

"'Cause it was a crazy bear," Lizzie put in.

"That's right." Jack went on in his storyteller voice. "That bear caused a lot of trouble. Then one morning, a settler's wife caught him raiding her chicken coop."

"What did she do?" Lizzie's eyes widened.

"Well, she didn't like it one bit that he was stealing her chickens. So she grabbed up the shotgun and filled his ornery old hide full of buckshot. He ran off and no one ever saw him again."

"Good for her." Ellin smiled at him over Lizzie's head.

"Never underestimate the wrath of a ticked-off pioneer woman."

Jack laughed. "Or any woman, for that matter. That's always been my policy."

"Oh, I get it," Lizzie said. "It's called Crazy Bear Holler 'cause the lady made the crazy bear holler."

Careful not to discount the little girl's conclusion, he explained that in Arkansas, the valleys between hills were known as hollows, but most people called them hollers.

"Does your sister's family live out here?" Ellin's tone clearly expressed her opinion of extreme living.

"No. They have a place in town. They plan to build a house here later, when the kids are older. Laurel's just a year old and they have a boy almost five."

"What's his name?" Lizzie asked.

"Colton. Maybe you'd like to play with him sometime."

"I might," she allowed. "Does he like princesses?"

"I'm sure he does."

"Does your sister work?" asked Ellin.

Jack nodded. "According to Jana, all mothers work. Besides taking care of the kids and the house, she has a bookkeeping and accounting business."

"Are her children in day care?"

"She leaves them with a lady in town. Mrs. Kendall."

"I'll need a sitter for Lizzie," Ellin said. "Ida Faye was planning to watch her, but that's out of the question for the time being. Do you think your sister would recommend someone?"

"I'll ask her. Or better yet, I'll introduce you, and you can ask her yourself." Jack wanted the two women to meet so his twin would see how wrong she was about Ellin. He had no doubt the self-assured woman beside him *could* be a pain if the occasion demanded, but he didn't think she actually *was* one. A small, but important, distinction.

"You've always lived in Washington?"

She gave the question an accusatory spin, like a cross-examining prosecutor. *So, Mr. Madden, you would have this court believe vanilla is the only ice cream flavor you've ever tasted?*

"Born and raised," he said with a sly challenge.

"I suppose you went to school locally, as well?"

*Come now, Mr. Madden, have you never been tempted to try chocolate? Or strawberry? What about Rocky Road?*

*Objection, Your Honor. Pressuring the witness.* "I earned a bachelor's degree at the University of Arkansas. I traveled a bit before completing postgraduate work at Stanford."

She looked skeptical, like she could produce DNA evidence to the contrary. "You have an advanced degree? From Stanford?"

Jack nodded solemnly. A less secure man might be affronted by her surprise, but he rather enjoyed it. "You'd be amazed at the number of closet educated people in Arkansas. Gotta protect that possum-eating hillbilly image Hollywood gave us."

"I intended no offense." Her pretty flush assured him she meant it.

"None taken." Jack had to watch the rugged road, but he glanced in her direction often. He enjoyed looking at Ellin Bennett, making little discoveries about her. Like the dimple that appeared at one corner of her mouth when she smiled a certain way. The tiny white scar that bisected the tip of her left brow. The canine that lapped ever so slightly over its neighbor. Getting to know her was akin to opening a brightly wrapped gift box and finding another one inside—a never-ending surprise. The suspense was killing him.

He'd already learned some interesting things about her.

She was an attentive mother. She actually said "holy-moley." She was city-bred but knew how to dress for a trip to the woods. And she was trying hard to conceal her nervousness. He suspected she was not often ill at ease, and it pleased him to think he made her fidget like a four-year-old.

He would have been sorely disappointed if she hadn't been tipped a little off-balance when she met him sans Santa suit. She needed to have her strong opinions challenged once in a while, and he believed he was just the man to do it.

He liked her hair down. Restrained by a skier's headband, it tumbled to her shoulders in glorious brown waves, as soft as he imagined and smelling of wildflowers. He tightened his hands on the steering wheel. Even on such a short acquaintance, he understood her well enough to know she would not appreciate him reaching over and sifting his fingers through the silky strands. But that was exactly what he wanted to do.

"You said you traveled after college. Any place in particular?"

"Africa." He didn't elaborate and hoped she wouldn't press for details.

"Really? And you decided to live here?"

*You claim you actually tried Rocky Road, Mr. Madden, and prefer vanilla? Yes, prosecutor. Guilty as charged.* "I like Washington. My friends are here, my family's here. I love my work. Why wouldn't I want to stay?"

She shrugged. "There's a whole world out there."

"Yep, and I'll stick with Washington. You sound like Jana. It's okay for her to settle down here, but she thinks I'm a slacker because I want to."

"I'm sure she doesn't think that."

Jack laughed. "She not only thinks it, she broadcasts it

to the public on a regular basis. I'm surprised she hasn't taken out an ad.'' He drew a banner headline in the air with one hand. "Jack Madden Is Not Fulfilling His Potential. Do you have brothers or sisters?''

She shook her head. "I'm an only child, born before mom realized how time-consuming motherhood would be. My parents divorced when I was ten.''

Insight based on teaching experience and intuition gave Jack a glimpse of Ellin as a little girl, lonely and desperate for parental attention. He'd seen it before. When the acceptance they craved wasn't forthcoming, some kids acted out. Others withdrew. The smart ones, the survivors, found comfort in achievement.

"Jana and I are twins," he said. "She thinks sharing a womb and being born first gives her squatter's rights on my destiny.''

"You two must be very close.''

He nodded. "Yeah, we are.'' It would be hard to explain twinship to someone without a sibling. He liked to complain about Jana's well-intentioned meddling, it was part of the game they played. But he couldn't imagine living without her or the other noisy, nosy members of his extended family.

"Your parents are here, I take it?''

"Yep. Hal and Mary. They run a chicken farm a few miles south of town. I'll have to show you two their operation sometime. It's all automated. Up to date. Very impressive.''

"I don't know.'' Ellin inclined her head in Lizzie's direction. "I'm afraid if she finds out where drumsticks and chicken nuggets really come from, she won't want to eat them.''

"They don't raise chickens for the packing plant,'' he said. "They sell eggs.''

"Oh, that's different. A trip to a real egg farm might be very educational."

"I recall Ida Faye saying your dad passed away a few years back, but what about your mother?"

"She finally left Chicago for Phoenix. Said she was tired of snow. She sells commercial real estate."

Interesting that she described her mother by occupation, as though what a person did for a living revealed the most about them. But that fit with what he'd heard about Ellin. She was more than just career-minded; getting ahead was more important to her than getting along.

Had her drive to succeed undermined her marriage? According to Ida Faye, it had ended more than two years ago. Before he could ask about it, Lizzie interrupted with another question.

"Do deers live in these woods?" She looked around hopefully.

"Sure, they do. Lots of them." Jack parked the truck in a small meadow dotted with young cedars. In the summertime the grass fairly glowed with yellow wildflowers, but now, a week before Christmas, it was dry and brown, limned by frost.

"Reindeers?"

"No. Just little whitetails."

"Can we see some?"

"Maybe. They come down to drink at the creek in the evening. We might see some there."

"Goody." Lizzie clapped her mittened hands at the prospect.

Ellin picked up the thread of their conversation as though trying to settle something in her mind. "You say you like it here and all, but haven't you ever just wanted, well, more?"

Jack switched off the engine. She seemed to think not

wanting more meant settling for less. He'd have to set her straight about that. He smiled as he turned to face her and cocked his elbow on the seat behind Lizzie.

"I never said I didn't want more." He caught her gaze and held it. "I do. I just don't happen to think I have to go somewhere else to find it."

Ellin watched fondly as Lizzie ran around the meadow like a puppy kept too long in a box. She flitted from one tree to the next, crying "How about this one?"

Jack had a way with her little girl. Carrying his ax Paul Bunyan-style over his sturdy shoulder, he followed her around, making a show of seriously considering each of her ill-advised choices. Even a twenty-foot-tall pine. He didn't talk down to her or discount her childish opinions. He asked questions that made her think. Then he guided her to logical conclusions.

And he made it all look effortless. Maybe his skill was a result of his teacher's training or dealing with children on a daily basis. Or maybe he was just a nice guy with a good heart. Whatever it was, it was certainly refreshing. She'd dated very little since her divorce, having finally decided she was not marriage material. The child-friendly men she met considered her too career-focused, and fellow workaholics resented the time she spent with her daughter.

Her ex-husband, Andrew, fell into the latter category. If he could relate to his only child as this stranger did, things might have turned out differently for their dysfunctional little family. If he had found joy in his daughter instead of viewing her as a noisome distraction, they might have overcome their other problems. If they'd found common ground as Lizzie's parents, maybe they wouldn't have had to compete in every other aspect of their lives.

Visitation was part of the divorce agreement, but her ex-husband expressed little interest in exercising that right.

She'd called him on it last year when he announced his move to Seattle. He'd shrugged it off, saying, "maybe in a few years when she's older and not so much bother." The selfish fool didn't seem to understand, or maybe he didn't care, that unlike having the tires rotated, bonding with a child wasn't something he could postpone until a more convenient time.

The tree hunters interrupted her thoughts. "And we have a winner!" Jack called out with game show host enthusiasm. He indicated their choice with a sweeping Vannaesque gesture.

Lizzie danced around the little cedar, setting the pom pom on the end of her stocking cap into motion. "Isn't it pretty, Mommy?"

"Yes, very," Ellin agreed. "Smells good, too."

"Yep. I picked it out all by myself." Lizzie turned to Jack who was waiting with ax in hand and issued one of her royal edicts. "Okay, you can start choppin' now."

He winked at Ellin. Then pretending to spit in his hands, he rubbed them together and swung the ax dramatically. After a few solid whacks, he yelled "Timber!" and the four-foot-tall tree toppled to the ground.

"This is my bestest Christmas tree ever," Lizzie pronounced over the fallen evergreen. She insisted on helping Jack carry it to the truck.

Ellin brought up the rear. She'd been right to come on this little jaunt, even if Jack's startling transformation from jolly old gentleman to sexy *young* hunk had rattled her. Lizzie was having the time of her life. The discomfort of her own reluctant physical awareness was a small price to pay for her little girl's giggles.

Besides, she was probably making too much of it. So what if Jack Madden lifted her spirits and made her heart beat a little faster? She hadn't been in a serious relationship for over two years. What felt like chemistry might just be hungry hormones yearning for action. Instant attraction wasn't reliable, nor was it always mutual.

Jack had been more attentive to Lizzie than to her. He hadn't said or done anything to make her think his interest was anything other than neighborly. And that was just the way she wanted it.

Right?

The expedition was a resounding success. Not only did they locate the perfect Christmas tree, Jack paused on the trip down the hill to point out a family of deer browsing in the brush. The wildlife sighting propelled Lizzie over the top, and her heartfelt declaration of "I *love* this place" gave Ellin something else to worry about: how her daughter would react in three months when it was time to leave.

It was dark by the time they returned to Ida Faye's. Jack carried the tree inside and clamped it into a metal stand while Ellin peeled Lizzie out of her snowsuit. Pudgy greeted them by bouncing around the living room, his yapper on full throttle.

Jack set the tree up in front of the picture window and Lizzie helped him fluff out the lacy branches. The scent of cedar soon filled the room.

"Can we decorate it now, Mommy? Can I put the angel on top? Can Jack help?"

"Oh, I think we've imposed long enough." Ellin stood behind her daughter, her hands on the thin shoulders as though using the child as a buffer between them. "We can't ask him to give up his entire evening. I'm sure he has other things to do."

Lizzie's upturned face swiveled from Ellin to Jack. "Do ya?"

He shook his head. "Nope. I'm free as a bird."

Lizzie turned back to her mother. "See. He can stay and

help me put the angel on top. I'm hungry. Can you cook some pasketti? Can Jack eat wif us? Huh, Mommy?''

Ellin groaned inwardly. This was not good. Jack was easy to talk to, and she'd been so lonely these past weeks. But the tree quest was taking on definite datelike dimensions, something she'd vowed to avoid. She didn't want him to stay but was even more reluctant to see him go. A dilemma if ever there was one.

Lizzie did not share her reservations. "Don't you want to eat wif us, Jack? Aren't ya hungry?''

"Well,'' he admitted, "I worked up quite an appetite with all that chopping.''

Lizzie beamed with satisfaction. "See? That means he's hungry, too. Go make pasketti now.''

Jack laughed. Ellin sighed in exasperation and made a rolling gesture of obeisance. "Yes, your Royal Munchkinness. Your wish is my command.''

"Okay.'' Lizzie ducked behind Ellin and pushed her into Ida Faye's little kitchen. Jack started to follow, but she latched on to his hand and pulled him toward the couch. "You stay in here and read me a story.''

"Yes, ma'am, princess.''

Ellin gave him an apologetic look. "Can you tell she's used to getting her way?''

"I'd say she comes by it naturally.''

"Can I take your coat?''

He slipped out of the dark blue seaman's jacket and handed it to her. Her heart thumped with another little thrill of appreciation. Just as she'd feared. There *was* a nice broad chest under the cable-knit sweater. And firm biceps. With his cold-burnished cheeks and wayward hair, he looked like that virile Old Spice sailor, home from the stormy sea. After a long voyage without female companionship and rife with desire.

Holey-moley. What was her problem? The guy was just being himself. Maybe that was the trouble. "I'll just be a little while." She headed for the kitchen before he could see how her own imagination affected her.

He glanced up from the couch where Lizzie had heaped her favorite picture books and smiled. Darn. Now he looked like a kindly Father Goose. Bad Ellin. She had to get those errant, needy thoughts under control.

"Take your time," he told her. "We have plenty to keep us busy out here."

She put pasta on to boil, then peeked into the living room. Jack sat with Lizzie snuggled comfortably in the crook of his arm, an open book on his lap. He was in the middle of a dramatic reading of *The Story of the Three Little Pigs* in which he somehow managed to make the Big Bad Wolf sound like a regular guy. How the heck did he do it?

After a simple dinner of spaghetti and salad, Jack helped Ellin carry the box of Christmas ornaments in from the garage. He sat in Ida Faye's recliner with a cup of coffee in his hand and Pudgy in his lap and watched the Bennett girls decorate their tree. He imagined Jana's reaction when she called for a full report of the day's events and found he still wasn't home. It would drive her nuts and serve her right.

Funny, he'd only known Ellin and Lizzie a few hours, and yet he felt strangely at ease. Being here with them gave him that familiar, déjà vu feeling that thrilled and frightened at the same time. He knew there was something right and logical about meeting them. Something fateful. As though the sequence of events that led them out of Chicago and into his life had been carefully orchestrated for his benefit.

Maybe this was it. He was startled by the notion at first,

but soon recognized it like a childhood friend, long missing and much desired. Ever since he'd first raised adolescent questions about the opposite sex, his father had assured him that when he met the woman he was meant to share his life with, he would know she was "The One." The tired old world would look new, like a garden after a summer rain. He wouldn't be able to imagine a future without her or remember a past that she wasn't part of. His old man had made him a promise. When the right woman came along, everything would change.

Who could be a more forceful agent of change than Ellin Bennett? Was she really "The One"? Maybe. The question had never come up in regard to any other woman, and Jack had figured his father for a romantic old fool of a chicken farmer. Who would have thought he might know what he was talking about?

He couldn't remember when he'd enjoyed himself more than he had today. He ruffled Pudgy's fur, feeling like a man with the key to his dreams in one hand and a ticking time bomb in the other. He didn't know what could happen between them, but he wanted to find out. However, in three short months Ellin and her little girl would be gone from his life. Unless he did something about it.

"This is my special angel." Lizzie held up a winged creature with abundant hair and a frilly dress. It looked more like a high-fashion doll than a celestial being. "She goes on the very toppest top."

"You did a good job decorating the tree," he told her. "Now you'll be ready when Santa comes."

"Cept we gots no chimbly," she said with a pout. "I don't think he can get in."

"Lizzie, we talked about that," Ellin reminded her gently. "Santa is magic. He doesn't need to come down the chimney."

But she was clearly worried. "I just wish we had one."

"Here," Jack distracted her. "Let me help you put that angel up there." He held her up, and she poked the tip of the cedar tree up the angel's skirt.

"Okay," he told her. "Sit on the couch with your mom."

She did as instructed, and he darkened the room by switching off the table lamps. Then he reached behind the tree and plugged in the strands of multicolored twinkle lights.

"Ooh!" Lizzie cooed. "It's bufutul."

Jack sat on the couch beside her. He wasn't looking at the Christmas tree, but at Ellin when he answered. "Yes. Very beautiful."

Later, Ellin came in from the kitchen with two cups of coffee and handed one to Jack. Lizzie was asleep in his lap, her long hair fanned over his arm.

"I'm sorry. She was really cranked up tonight." She moved to take the sleeping child, but he waved her away.

"Leave her. I don't mind." He stroked Lizzie's hair as he sipped his coffee.

"You're good with kids," she said. "Believe it or not, she doesn't warm up this fast to just anyone."

"I like children. I wouldn't be a teacher if I didn't."

"I don't imagine it pays very well. Especially in a town this size."

He shrugged. "Don't you know? With all the intrinsic rewards teachers receive for molding young minds, it would be just plain greedy of us to expect a decent salary, too."

She was pretty sure he was teasing, but it was hard to tell with him. "Well, anyway, you made quite an impression on the princess. Both as Santa and as Jack."

"What can I say? Kids like me. Dogs, too." He glanced

at Pudgy curled up beside him. "I think it's because they're such astute judges of character."

She laughed. "Let me know if you ever need a baby-sitting job."

"Actually I sit with my niece and nephew all the time."

"Really?"

"Does that surprise you?"

It wasn't hard to do so. Worldly in many ways, Ellin actually knew very little about men. She never quite understood them, so their actions often took her by surprise. Jack was no exception. But unlike those of other men, his surprises were invariably pleasant. With a touch of the too-good-to-be-true thrown in to confuse her even further. "I don't think Lizzie's father ever changed a diaper."

"Is that why you're not together anymore?"

"That and a million other reasons I won't go into at the moment."

"Fair enough." He finished the coffee and set the cup on the table. "Tell me about yourself instead."

"What do you mean?"

"Don't be so suspicious. Sharing personal information is a socially acceptable way for two people to get to know each other. But if it's a problem just pretend I'm the English teacher and you're giving an oral book report on *The Life and Times of Ellin Bennett*."

"I'm afraid it would be a boring tale."

"Let me be the judge of that."

She meant to just tell him how she got into journalism. Work was a good, neutral subject, one she felt comfortable with. But he was an attentive listener, and she hadn't had anyone to talk to for a very long time. She found herself sharing details of her dismissal from the Chicago paper. She told him about the unverified story that had made a public laughingstock out of an Illinois state representative who wouldn't back down until her superiors handed him her head on a figurative platter.

"Their official stance was that I was grossly incompetent." She tried to keep the bitterness out of her voice. "I'm not. I was tired. I was in a hurry. I was careless. But I'm not incompetent. I'm an excellent journalist."

"I never doubted it," he told her. "Why did you agree to come here?"

"Ida Faye told me about the job and set up the interview with Jig Baker. I could have gotten a position somewhere else, I guess. But I needed a time-out. A safe place to lick my wounds and nurse my pride. It seemed like a good idea. I have three months to decide what to do with the rest of my life."

"Then what?" he prompted.

"Then? Who knows? I'll send out some résumés, call some people, see what happens."

"In the meantime…"

"In the meantime I'll do a good job at the *Post-Ette*."

"I'm sure you will." He pulled a crocheted afghan off the back of the couch and arranged it carefully over Lizzie.

"I'll admit I wasn't exactly thrilled about coming here."

"It felt like coming down in the world?" he guessed.

"Let's just say I've been climbing up so long it became a habit. Washington, Arkansas, seemed like a step in the wrong direction." More like a fall off Mt. Everest, but she couldn't tell him that.

"I understand."

"But I plan to give it a hundred percent. I'll work hard."

"Not too hard, I hope."

"What?"

"This isn't Chicago. It's more chicken peck chicken than dog eat dog here. Things don't move as fast as you're used to."

"Tell me about it. There's only one parking meter on Main Street. What's up with that?" She sipped the last of her lukewarm coffee.

He laughed. "Back in the seventies, the city council decided to try an experiment. They wanted to find out if parking meters would generate enough revenue to pay for themselves and make the city treasury some money."

"So what happened?"

"They only had funds budgeted for one so they had it installed. The problem was, nobody parked there. After a few months the town fathers declared the parking meter experiment a monumental failure and tabled the issue."

She looked at him in consternation. "That's absurd. Didn't they realize that as long as there were no meters at the other spaces, no one would park where they had to pay?"

"You would think."

"They should have used money from the general fund to install meters at every parking space. Then they could have mandated a portion of the city sales tax to repay the—"

"Ellin?"

"Yeah?"

"That's not how we do things here."

"But that would have been a good plan—"

"Ellin?"

"Yes?"

"This isn't Chicago."

"I've noticed. Sometimes I feel like I've stepped into a black-and-white episode of The Andy Griffith Show. In an alternative universe where there is no pizza delivery."

"Around here, eating out is a social activity. We pack up the kids, go to Mama Maria's, play pool, visit with our friends and make an evening of it. Who wants to order a solitary pizza and eat it alone?''

She admitted there was logic in that. "But how do you manage without a twenty-four-hour grocery store?"

"We plan ahead."

"And only one movie screen."

"We try to muddle through. We get a new movie every week."

Her face lit up. Now she had him. "There's no mall."

"And we call ourselves a town." He smacked his forehead with mock derision. "The shame of it all."

"You're making fun of me, Jack Madden," she accused. With very little effort, he made her feel shallow and spoiled for considering such material luxuries her due.

"I'd never do that, Ellin Bennett."

His words were spoken as softly as a lover's caress. For a crazy moment, she longed for his touch on her skin, the brush of his full lips against hers. She was mesmerized by a need so intense it caused a physical ache.

Holy guacamole! What was she thinking? "It's getting late. I need to put Lizzie to bed." She stood up and leaned over to lift her sleeping daughter from his arms. She heard his sharp intake of breath when her hair swung down and brushed his cheek.

Her eyes met his. For one heart-stopping moment she knew he meant to kiss her. And she was stunned to realize how much she wanted him to.

Instead, he broke the electric connection between them by lifting Lizzie, afghan and all, into her arms.

She hefted her child to her shoulder and started for the bedroom on trembling legs. It wasn't the prospect of Jack kissing her that made her knees wobbly. Or even that she would have kissed him back. No. What had shaken her was the disappointment she felt when he didn't.

"Ellin?" he called softly.

"Yes?" She didn't turn around. She could not let him see how deeply the encounter had affected her.

"I think I should let myself out."

"Yes," she agreed in a breathless whisper. "That's what I was thinking."

## Chapter Four

Jack stopped by Jana's office the next morning to drop off the key he'd borrowed. She planned to close between Christmas Eve and New Year to be with family and gear up for the coming tax season. Surely, she would be busy. With a little luck, he could toss the key through the door, thank her on the fly for the Bennetts' Christmas tree and escape before his sister morphed into the Grand Inquisitor.

He never had much luck.

"I'm not exactly happy with you, mister." She looked up from an open ledger and drew a you-are-dead-meat line across her throat with a pencil.

"What'd I do now?"

"Nothing. That's the problem. I waited up until midnight last night. I'm the mother of two small children. I cannot afford to lose sleep for no reason. Why didn't you call me?"

"I wasn't aware it was check-in day. Or that you were filling in for my parole officer." A lifetime of trying to out-quip his sibling had taught him when to fold. He flipped her the key which she caught with a deft movement. Sitting in a chair across from her, he leaned back, his hands stuffed into the pockets of his jacket.

"Come on, Jack. If I had spent the whole afternoon and evening alone with the good-looking new guy in town, you know you'd want to hear every dirty little detail."

He frowned and pushed his wire-rims up with one finger. "And so would your poor cuckolded husband, I would imagine."

"You know what I mean." She closed the ledger with a snap. "What's going on here?"

Feigning exaggerated interest, he looked around the quiet little office decorated with his nephew Colton's crayoned masterpieces. "Nothing at the moment. But sharpen your pencils, Sis. You never know when there'll be an accounting emergency."

She made a face that told him how impossible she thought he was and filled two mugs from the coffee pot on the credenza. "Did she put any big city moves on you? Or take advantage of your callow country naïveté? Give it up, Bro! Did you, or did you not, engage in anything even remotely resembling hanky-panky last night?"

Jack curled his fist to his forehead in a pose reminiscent of Rodin's *The Thinker*. "How many angels can dance on the head of a pin? What is the one true meaning of life? Why does toast always fall butter side down? Oh, the irony of unanswerable questions."

"Nobody likes a smart-aleck, little brother."

"I thought it was, nobody likes a busybody."

"So you're not talking?"

"Not about me and Ellin Bennett. Now, if you want to discuss the role of symbolism in nineteenth-century American literature, I'm your man."

"You and Ellin? Ha!" Jana's dark eyes, so like his own,

sparked with triumph. "So something did happen. I knew it. You can't fool me, you never could."

He leaned back and clasped his hands behind his head. "I'm thinking of inviting them for Christmas." He'd made up his mind last night on the way home. That almost-kiss and the memory of Ellin's lush, peach-colored lips had him hungry for more. More time together. More physical contact. More everything.

"Them who?"

"Ellin, her daughter and Ida Faye. Do you think Mom would object to having three extras for dinner?"

"Are you kidding? Mom patented the concept of 'The More the Merrier.' You think they'll come?"

"Won't know until I ask." But first he had to figure out the best way to approach Ellin. He might be eager to explore all the possibilities their slow-burn chemistry promised, but she'd be less than receptive. She was a stubborn cynic whose romantic notions needed some gentle tweaking. It would take a serious effort, but Jack felt he was up to the job. Problem was, he only had three months to work some magic and couldn't afford to make any dumb mistakes.

"What're you waiting for?" Jana pushed the phone toward him across the desk, much as she'd pushed the wriggling green caterpillar he'd had to eat when he was ten. The experience had taught him not to make wagers with his sister unless he was willing to pay the price.

"I said I was *thinking* about it." His half-baked plan did not allow for rash acts. He needed a sure-fire refusal-proof invitation.

She flapped her elbows like wings. "Bock-Bock-Bock."

Jana had challenged him with her stupid poultry imitation since elementary school. Unfortunately, he'd never been man enough to resist it. He gave her a resigned look and reached for the phone, then realized he didn't know Ida Faye's number. She read his mind and tossed the directory, which was the size of a small magazine, into his lap.

"Go for it, big guy." She studied him from several angles as he punched in the numbers. "And get a decent haircut, why don't you?"

The timer buzzed a shrill accusation. Ellin switched it off, grabbed the pot holders and pulled two pumpkin pies out of the oven. She grimaced as she set them on the cooling racks. They were way browner than any pumpkin pie she'd ever seen, but the middles were definitely jiggly. Who was she trying to impress with her culinary skills? She should have gone with her first impulse and bought ready-mades, but it was too late now. The bakery closed at noon on Christmas Eve.

Betty Crocker felt no compulsion to report news or edit copy. Why did Ellin Bennett think she could bake pies?

"What are they, Mommy?" Lizzie climbed up on a stool to check out the overcooked, underdone pastry experiment.

"Pumpkin pies, princess."

"Do *I* like pun'kin pie?"

"You did last year."

She wrinkled her nose. "I don't think I will this year."

"Yeah. I know what you mean." Ellin blew a loose strand of hair out of her face and wondered where she'd gone wrong. She'd followed Ida Faye's recipe, but hadn't really had her mind on the task. She'd been too busy fuming over being manipulated yet again. She still couldn't believe Jack Madden had fast-talked her into having Christmas dinner with him and his family.

Lizzie had been down for a nap when he called, and she'd been in a frustrated fizz trying to assemble the gajillion-piece dollhouse that topped her little girl's Christmas list. If she could only figure out which of the four hundred tabs was actually Tab A and which of the three hundred and ninety-nine slots was truly Slot B. She was mentally composing an editorial admonishing lawmakers to make it illegal for non-English speakers to write assembly instructions when the phone rang. She'd lunged for it to keep from waking her sleeping child.

It had been that wiseacre elf impersonator. The first thing he'd said was, "Wow, I had no idea just hearing my voice would leave you so breathless." She hadn't even bothered to explain. He'd made his pitch, and she'd politely refused. However, negative responses didn't seem to register with the man. He finally wore her down by asking if she really wanted Lizzie to spend Christmas Day with the old folks at Shady Acres, quietly eating turkey off a tray in an institutional setting?

Wouldn't she prefer his parents' rambling farm where there was room to run and explore, children to play with, kittens to cuddle? Surely her grandmother would enjoy an outing with old friends after being confined to the nursing home? And Ellin could meet his extended family, which happened to make up a sizable portion of the town's population and newspaper readership. This was her big chance to prove once and for all that Chicagoans were not an alien species.

Honestly. She'd tried to say no.

"Mommy?" Lizzie's insistent arm-patting pulled her out of her thoughts.

"Yes?"

"Somebody's at the door."

Ellin had to dance around Pudgy who always knew exactly where she planned to step next and somehow managed to get there first. "Watch it, will you? You want *me* to fall and break a hip?"

She wiped her hands on her grandmother's apron and smoothed her hair, reaching the front door just as Lizzie tugged it open with both hands.

"Hi, Jack!" Her daughter was obviously happier to see their unannounced visitor than she was. Lizzie wrapped her arms around his legs, and he stooped to give her a hug.

"Hey, princess." He straightened and smiled. "Ellin."

"Madden." She wondered if she looked as perspiry as she felt and swiped her sweaty palms on her apron. She stepped back, and he walked in, his coat collar turned up against the wind, his hair in worse disarray than usual. It always looked as though he'd just crawled out of bed. Which made her think of cold winter nights snuggled under warm flannel sheets, pressed up against bare, musky male flesh.

Jeez! What was the matter with her? Since when had pumpkin pie spice become an aphrodisiac?

"You were expecting Santa Claus maybe?" Without warning, he reached out and rubbed her chin gently with his thumb.

Surprised by the unexpected contact, Ellin stepped back and nearly tripped over Pudgy. With an amazing display of reflexes, Jack grabbed her to correct her balance. His touch burned through her sweater, and her skin tingled. She felt an inexplicable urge to hurl herself against him, just to experience that incredible sensation all over. Holy-moley! Did she need to get a grip or what? No man had ever gotten to her the way this guy did, and she didn't like it one bit.

No, that wasn't true. She liked it a little too much.

"You had a dab of flour there." His lingering gaze began a leisurely tour, starting with her lopsided ponytail and traveling over the ruffled apron, down to the funny bunny slippers on her feet. Then taking its sweet time, it worked its way up again.

His sexy grin and open appreciation of her disheveled self made Ellin's hair roots throb. Which had to be the dumbest trick her body had ever played on her. "I'm kind of in the middle of something." She waved her arm absently toward the kitchen, hoping to conceal her reaction behind a show of impatience. "You're early. It's not Christmas yet, is it?"

"No."

"So you just stopped by to…?"

He sniffed the air and frowned. "Is something burning?"

"No." She didn't want him to know she'd ruined her contribution to tomorrow's dinner.

"Mommy's baking." To Lizzie, it was the only explanation needed.

"And I should get back to it."

"I just came by to give Lizzie something," he said.

"A present for me?" Lizzie jumped up and down and tugged on his coat. "What is it?"

Jack reached in his pocket, pulled out a small tissue paper package and handed it to her. "Santa Claus wanted me to make sure you got this."

She ripped off the wrapping and held up an old-fashioned skeleton key. It had been sprayed with glittery gold paint and threaded with a red velvet ribbon to which a small bell and piece of holly were attached.

"What's it for?" she asked with a puzzled look.

He knelt on one knee to achieve her level. "Remember how you were worried that Santa won't be able to get in the house because there's no chimney for him to come down?"

"Yes." Lizzie turned the fancy key over in her small hands.

"Well, that's one of Santa's magical keys. All you have to do is hang the ribbon outside on the doorknob tonight before you go to bed. When Santa comes, he'll use it to open the door and put your presents under the tree. But it only works for Santa Claus. No one else."

"Really?" Lizzie's blue eyes were wide with Christmas magic.

"Truly."

"Oh, thank you, Jack." She hugged his neck, and Ellin envied her daughter's inhibition to do so. "I'm glad you're Santa's special friend. And mine, too."

"Why don't you hang it on the Christmas tree for safe-keeping until later?"

Lizzie draped the ribbon over one of the cedar's branches, then flopped down on the floor to rearrange the gifts underneath.

"Thank you," Ellin said.

"You're welcome."

"Did you make it yourself?"

He nodded. "I thought it would help her get to sleep tonight."

"It will." Her eyes narrowed. "Does Martha Stewart know about you?"

"Where do you think I got the idea?"

"You really don't have enough to do now that school's out for the holidays, do you?"

"I have a few projects planned."

His tone made her think she might be one of those projects. She wanted to tell him to beat it before she did something she would regret. And he could just forget about tomorrow. There was nothing wrong with eating turkey off a tray at Shady Acres. But all she could think of was how he'd taken the time to spray glitter on a thrift store key to make her little girl happy.

"It was really nice of you," she said grudgingly.

"I'm quite a likable guy, once you get to know me."

That was exactly the problem. He *was* likable. Thoughtful. Generous. Cute. A regular hometown hero. Jack Madden was a big, adorable fish in an itty-bitty pond. A safe little tide pool she would inhabit for ninety days before plunging back into the dark, shark-infested ocean of real life. She couldn't afford to like him too much. It would only make the sharks she was used to seem more annoying.

He opened the door, stepped out onto the porch and propped one hand against the jamb. "I'll pick you two up tomorrow. Then we'll head over to Shady Acres for Ida Faye. Eleven o'clock still good for you?"

"Eleven o'clock is fine."

"Okay, then." He reached out again, this time drawing a slow finger along her cheek. "Goodbye, Ellin Bennett."

She closed the door, leaned against it and fanned her flushed face with her apron. She was amazed she couldn't come up with a single legitimate excuse to avoid spending the day with such an emotionally provoking man. Back in Chicago she could have pleaded a work emergency. A pressingly tight schedule. A killer deadline. There was never a shortage of newsworthy distractions.

Crooked cops, corrupt politicians, addicted celebrities. Banks robbed and homes burgled. Arsonists bent on honing their craft. Accidents snarling traffic and creating delays. There was always something urgent demanding her attention, filling up her days and her life.

But not here. She had too much time on her hands. Things would be different once she started at the *Post-Ette*. She obviously didn't know how to function without the pressure of work. How else could she explain the sudden urge to bake pies? Clearly, inactivity was to blame for her being confused and unsettled and ready to jump out of her skin when a man she'd known less than a week touched her.

She'd been too long in the trenches to feel comfortable on the home front. Didn't wartime research prove that rest and recreation took the edge off battle-hardened veterans and made them more vulnerable to brainwashing tactics?

The outside of Hal and Mary Madden's two-storied Victorian farmhouse was decorated with white twinkle lights and pine wreaths. Inside, it overflowed with relatives and friends. Everyone, adults and children alike, was full of good will and Christmas cheer. Mouth-watering aromas wafted through the homey, country-style rooms. Roasting turkey. Baking ham. Sweet potatoes. Cinnamon and nutmeg and hot apple cider. An elaborately decorated tree dominated the bay window. Pine and cedar garlands wound up the banister and trailed off the mantel. Perry Como and Andy Williams crooned carols from record albums stacked on the spindle of an old-fashioned console stereo.

Jack introduced Ellin to so many people she soon gave up trying to remember their names, hoping instead to keep the relationships straight: aunts, uncles, cousins, neighbors, boyhood friend, third grade teacher. Without exception, they made her feel welcome.

Jack's mother Mary was a tall, sturdy-looking woman in her fifties. She wore a perpetual smile and was living proof of the benefits of outdoor activity. She gave Ellin a welcoming hug, graciously accepting the plate of cookies hurriedly baked from refrigerated dough to replace the ruined pies. Ellin was a bit embarrassed when she placed it on a sideboard alongside desserts fancy enough to make a French pastry chef jealous.

Jack led her into the paneled family room. A group of older men were gathered around a card table for a game of hearts before the midafternoon meal. Jack introduced his father, a friendly, ruddy-faced farmer dressed in a white shirt and clean, creased denim overalls. At the other end of the room, the younger crowd watched a televised football game.

Ida Faye knew most of those present and greeted them by name. The fact that Ellin was her only granddaughter seemed to be all the endorsement she needed. She'd expected to feel like an outsider, unfamiliar with rural customs and traditions, but the Madden clan was warm and welcoming.

The big, airy kitchen was filled with women, young and old, stirring pots and tossing salads as they visited and caught up on one another's lives. Ida Faye was feeling exceptionally well for an octogenarian with a recently riveted hip. In a couple of weeks she'd be discharged from the care center to continue her physical therapy at home. She staked out a spot at the table next to another elderly matron, and they joined forces to supervise a small group of children decorating cookies with colored icing and sprinkles. They invited Lizzie to join in, and she soon had more frosting on her face than on the sugary star she was working on.

Ellin looked around with unconcealed wonder. She hadn't seen so many people working this smoothly to put on a meal since she'd covered a national caterers' convention. Pots and saucepans bubbled on the stove. Bowls and platters and casserole dishes filled with delicious-looking food covered the counters. Napkin-lined baskets held warm, crusty rolls. So much abundance. How would it all ever be eaten?

The house was as full of happiness as it was the scents, sights and sounds of Christmas. From the beribboned wreath on the front door to the child-made decorations on the tree, it was obvious to Ellin that this close-knit brood valued holiday traditions. She was grateful to them for sharing this special day with her little family.

She thought about her own childhood when she couldn't get up before ten o'clock on Christmas morning because her mother liked to sleep late. Her mother didn't have time to cook so they ate their holiday meals in restaurants. They never had a real tree because her mother said the needles made a mess. Her mother put away the ornaments Ellin made at school because they weren't "nice" enough to hang on the tree. She bought cookies in a bag at the store. It was years before Ellin realized other people baked at home. She tried to recall if they had ever observed traditions, but all she could remember were the inevitable fights her parents had when she was young, and later, the loneliness she felt when her father left.

Why hadn't she been allowed to spend time in Arkansas with her grandmother? Was her mother afraid she might discover what was missing in her life? Or was it just another way to punish her father? She wondered if Andrew would ever want Lizzie for the holidays, and how she would feel if he did.

She smiled at Lizzie who didn't know the meaning of the word shy. She'd taken an immediate liking to Jack's five-year-old nephew, Colton. When they finished icing cookies, they were absorbed into the boisterous gang of children playing with new Christmas toys in the downstairs rec room. Jack assured her there were plenty of responsible preteen second cousins around to keep an eye on the younger kids.

His sister was one of the last people he introduced. The young woman was setting plates around the lace-covered table in the dining room while balancing an apple-cheeked infant on her hip. "Ellin, this is my sister Jana and little

Laurel." He kissed the baby's dark hair. "Jana's been dying to meet you."

"Yes, I have." Grinning at her brother, she stuck out her hand, and Ellin gave it a businesslike shake. "I'm so glad you could come. Jack hasn't stopped talking about you."

Ellin sensed the current of good-natured competition zinging between the siblings. Even without the introduction, she would have known Jana was Jack's twin. Long-legged like her brother, she had a trim, athletic figure. Her face was heart-shaped and pretty, without all the interesting angles that made his so masculine. Her hair, cut in a chin-length bob, was a matching shade of brown, her dark eyes just as lively. Openly assessing, Jana seemed satisfied with whatever snap judgments she'd reached about the newcomer.

"So Ellin, how do you like Washington so far?" She jostled the baby who was playing peekaboo with Jack. Without so much as a glance in his direction, Jana reached out and smacked her brother's hand when he tried to filch a cranberry from a bowl on the table.

"I like what I've seen. It seems like a nice little town."

"Oh, it is. Maybe not as stimulating as you're used to, but life in the slow lane does have advantages."

"I'm sure it does."

"I don't think you'll be bored here." She spoke to Ellin, but looked pointedly at Jack who popped a purloined berry into his mouth. "In fact, you might find your stay downright exciting."

"Maybe so. I want to thank you for letting us cut a tree from your property. Lizzie was so excited. It was her very first do-it-yourselfer."

"You're more than welcome. Glad my brother could be

such a big help." She placed unnecessary emphasis on the last word.

"Later, if you have time, I'd like to talk to you about child care. Jack thought you might recommend someone."

"Heck, I can introduce you to my sitter. She's planning to stop by after dinner for dessert and coffee. She's great with the kids. You'll love her."

"That would be super. I appreciate it."

"No problem." Jana looked from Jack to Ellin, and back again. She gave them a triumphant little smile and punched him lightly on the arm. "Yep, I think the next three months are going to be very interesting."

They were leaving the room when Jana called out for them to wait. They stopped under the arched doorway and Jack turned to his sister with a questioning look.

Jana just grinned and pointed to the woodwork above their heads with one extended finger.

Ellin looked up and saw the clump of mistletoe dangling at the end of a red ribbon. She gave an uneasy chuckle, certain this was one tradition she would not be asked to observe. Not even Jack Madden was that bold.

He frowned at his sister and let out a long, exasperated sigh. He shrugged one shoulder in a so-what gesture, and Jana flapped her free elbow and mouthed what appeared to be a chicken taunt. Ellin was no lip reader, but the meaning was clear. She was so caught up in the silent eye-play between the twins, that she didn't see the next move coming.

Before she could protest, escape or swoon, Jack dusted his hands with resolute determination, grabbed her shoulders, lowered his lips to hers and planted one on her. There was no other way to describe the firm, sensual command he took of the situation.

When he was finished, he urged Ellin from the room without so much as a backward glance at his startled sister, and sat her down at the bottom of the stairs to explain what had just happened.

"I'm sorry about that. It's certainly not how I planned our first kiss to be. Jana can be so immature at times."

Ellin was deep into lip shock from the heated encounter, but his choice of words caught her attention. *Planned? First kiss!*

"Excuse me?" She hoped she sounded sufficiently incredulous. There were too many people around to raise her voice, so she had to rely on an indignant whisper. "What's that supposed to mean? Calling something The First indicates a belief that more will follow. No way! That might have been the first, but it was also the *last!* So you can just forget whatever *plans* you think you have." She didn't bother with sheesh-the-nerve-of-some-people. It was implied in her tone.

He gave her an infuriating smile. Probably the same one he used on students who whined, "Gee, Mr. Madden, you can't give me an F on *Silas Marner*. What'll Coach say?" He was indulgent and kind. But clearly unwilling to be influenced by puny protests.

"Okay." His response to her tirade was even more unnerving.

She was cranking up for another run at it when she realized he had just agreed with her. "What does that mean? Okay?"

He pushed his glasses up his nose. "I'm not the kind of man who forces himself on a woman. I don't go in for caveman tactics. So okay."

"Just like that?" She did not trust him, he was too sneaky. "You mean you're giving up on, well, whatever it was you were thinking might happen between us?"

"I never said that."

"What then?"

"I agreed to forget my plan. Obviously, if you're not stewing in a state of anxious anticipation for our *next* kiss, it must not be working."

"Oh." He would forget it then. That was what she wanted to hear. So why did she feel so disappointed?

He stood up and pulled her to her feet. "I see now that what I really need is a *better* plan."

## Chapter Five

Ellin reported for editorial duty on the Monday after New Year's Day. Deanie Sue Mason, the paper's office manager and bookkeeper, welcomed her on board. The longtime widow told Ellin to help herself to coffee and if she needed anything else to just holler. Then she switched on the space heater aimed at her feet, parked her reading glasses on her nose and began sorting the morning mail.

Ellin walked to the back of the room and the oak floorboards creaked with each step. She sat down at the editor's cluttered desk which was a wasteland of correspondence, sticky notes and unlabeled file folders. How did he ever get anything done amid such chaos? She immediately started sorting through the litter in an attempt to whip it into order. Once she had the jumbled papers stacked, she opened the deep drawer on the side of the desk and stuffed them into a hanging file that she neatly labeled ''Baker's Desktop.''

She kneed the drawer closed with a good-riddance shudder and sipped her coffee as she surveyed the small office where she would spend the next three months. After the modern chrome, glass and steel of her Chicago workplace, the *Post-Ette* headquarters seemed more like a tableau from the Journalism Museum of History than a real newsroom. The computers almost seemed anachronistic.

It was located in a glass-fronted building on Main Street, which in Washington, ran barely three blocks. A high counter with an old-fashioned lift-up pass-through divided the reception area from the employees-only section. Deanie Sue's desk, freighted with plants, bean-stuffed animals and framed photos of her grandchildren, faced the front. The smell of ink and old paper permeated the room.

Tall green file cabinets lined one putty-colored wall. Pictures of former presidents Eisenhower, Kennedy and Clinton were aligned above them. Two antique fans hung from the ceiling, their dusty blades stilled for the winter.

On the other side of the room, floor-to-ceiling bookcases held binders of yellowing newspapers, the oldest pre-dating World War I. A moth-eaten mounted deer head stared down from the wall over the front door. Between Bambi and Rudolph, Ellin wondered if she would ever feel completely comfortable under its cross-eyed gaze.

The third full-time staffer, Owen Larsen, came in mumbling a red-faced greeting. He filled a coffee mug optimistically emblazoned with red script that spelled out Sixty is Sexy, and ducked his white head into the workroom in back. According to the owner, he had begun his career as a typesetter, but had managed to learn computer layout and printing techniques when the equipment was updated. Even though he was extremely shy, Ellin figured he would have to talk to her sooner or later, but it might not be today.

Ellin had met with owner/editor Jig Baker twice before his departure for Peru. Mostly he'd talked about archaeology and how lucky he was to have a chance to pursue his amateur interests on an official university-sponsored dig. But he'd also outlined her duties, assuring her that even though she was responsible for gathering news and writing copy, selling and laying out ads, proofing and correcting the prelims before they went to print, and overseeing mail-out distribution each Wednesday, she would rarely be required to work more than five or six hours per day.

She straightened a teetering pile of last week's papers and sighed. That left eighteen or nineteen hours to fill each day. She could sleep six or seven of those and spend a few more eating and taking care of life's little details. She could lavish time and attention on her daughter and grandmother, yet several hours remained open and unclaimed. Throughout her adult life, she'd never had that much discretionary time. She grimaced at the thought. Talk about a potential systems meltdown.

She could learn to crochet and bake a proper piecrust, or she could use the time productively. Since she wasn't cut out to be a domestic goddess, her top priority would be polishing her résumé and getting it out to prospective employers. She'd have to put a positive spin on the whole fired-for-incompetency incident, but she was a journalist. Tweaking an event for damage control didn't pose much of a problem.

The next three months would go by quickly, and her peace of mind required she have an acceptable position lined up well in advance. Unemployment and twenty-four unstructured hours a day was a nightmarish possibility that she wouldn't even consider.

At least now that school was back in session Jack Madden was occupied elsewhere most of the time, and she didn't have to deal with him on a regular basis. He'd been completely insufferable Christmas Day. A regular Mr. Congeniality. After their head-on lip collision under the mistletoe, he had acted as though nothing out of the ordinary had happened. Either he had been responding to his sister's dare, or the kiss simply had not affected him the way it had her. Most likely he'd just been hard at work, flipping her switches again.

After the bountiful dinner, she'd thanked her host and hostess for a wonderful day and told the rest of the Madden clan goodbye. Jack had been the soul of Southern charm, carefully avoiding any mention of their close encounter or his so-called plan. Unfortunately, Ellin couldn't think of anything else.

After a leisurely drive around town to admire the outdoor holiday decorations, they dropped a very tired Ida Faye off at Shady Acres. Jack drove to the little house on Dogwood Street where he promptly surprised Ellin by declining Lizzie's invitation to come in and see her new doll house. His parting shot was straight out of Clement Moore's famous poem, "Merry Christmas to all and to all a good night."

He'd climbed into his shiny red truck and disappeared into the cold dark, leaving Ellin with a head full of sleep-disturbing questions and lips that actually ached for another one of his stupid kisses. She should be glad he hadn't contacted her for over a week. Actually, she was grateful. The man was a menace. She had no idea what the heck he thought he was doing, but she would not let him manipulate her again. He obviously derived great pleasure in driving her crazy; she did not have to make it so darned easy for him.

Ellin removed a photo of Lizzie from her purse and set the wooden frame on her desk. After talking to Jana and meeting her sitter, she'd made child care arrangements with Mrs. Kendall, who agreed to watch Lizzie along with the two McGovern children. When she dropped her off this morning she'd expected a full-blown "mommy special," that just-right combination of tears, entreaties and quivering lower lip that induced guilt and made her question her maternal decision-making skills.

Instead, Lizzie had scampered away to play with Colton with no more than a quick smooch and a casual wave goodbye. Ellin had been prepared for an emotional siege and when none came, she was tipped even further off-balance. She should be pleased her daughter was adapting so well to her new environment, but she couldn't stop worrying how she'd react to another move when the time came.

"Did you find the story Jig wrote for you?" Deanie Sue asked. "I believe he left it in the middle desk drawer."

Ellin rifled through the drawer's contents until she located a folded sheet of paper with the words "Next Week's Lead" scribbled across it in red ink. She opened it, scanned the header, then looked up and smiled.

"This is a joke, right? Uh-huh. I get it. You're pulling my leg because it's my first day on the job." The story had to be the journalistic equivalent of a snipe hunt in the dark.

Deanie Sue, who had yet to exhibit anything resembling a sense of humor, insisted it was no joke.

"Dead Hog in Ditch Creates Controversy," Ellin read aloud. "You call that serious?"

The older woman nodded. "As a bad case of hives."

"I don't see how a dead hog can do anything, much less cause controversy."

"It's all the e in black and white," Deanie Sue told her. "Jig said it's the biggest thing to happen around here in ages. He said it could have significant repercussions. Especially in an election year."

Yeah, right. Ellin read the story about a large hog that had wandered onto the road outside of town. It was struck a glancing blow by a passing vehicle and staggered several yards before rolling into a ditch where it promptly gave up the ghost. Although decomposition of the estimated eight-hundred-pound carcass was hampered by cold temperatures, the rigor-mortised corpse was a public eyesore and the city council received numerous calls requesting its removal. They declined to do so, claiming the hog had expired just outside city limits, and referred callers to county officials.

Ellin shook her head and sighed. Considering the dramatic events unfolding elsewhere in the world, this hardly seemed worthy of the front page. But the *Post-Ette* could not afford to subscribe to the expensive wire services and so it only published stories of local interest.

She finished reading. Apparently, the county representative had investigated the matter and determined that while the hog may have collapsed beside a county road, it had most certainly been struck while still within city limits. Therefore, the accident was a town matter and the county could not intervene. Local law enforcement had been notified, but since no crime had been committed they had no incentive to become involved. So far, attempts to locate the hog's owner had proved fruitless as no one wanted to claim responsibility for the now "controversial" hog's removal.

Ellin tried to keep a straight face as she read aloud the last line of the story Baker had written. "In life the anonymous swine had no greater destiny than to grace the table in the form of pork chops and bacon. In death, it has achieved ignobility by becoming a bone of political contention."

Ignobility? She put down the article and shook her head. "This goes beyond absurd. This is plain silly."

"Not to the folks living in the area," Deanie Sue said knowingly. "If the weather warms up, it'll get downright smelly."

"So why doesn't someone just get rid of it?" Ellin asked. "End of story."

Owen peeked out of the back room. He swallowed hard and stared at the floor while asserting his opinion. "It ain't no easy thing to haul off a hog that big. I reckon a man would have to take a chain saw to it and take it out piece by piece. Messy business."

Ellin shuddered. "To say nothing of gruesome."

"Then he'd have to dig a hole and bury it," Owen went on.

"And it'd have to be a *big* hole. That ain't no road-killed coon you're talking about."

Ellin tackled the problem with her usual head-on approach. "Before we print this story, I'm going out there to see if it's been removed. If it's still there, I'll take photos and make some calls to see what can be done." She made a note of the location so she could drive to the scene before picking up Lizzie. "I'll get official statements from the mayor and city council members, then contact someone at the state level. Who's the representative for this district?"

When no one answered, Ellin looked up and found Deanie Sue and Owen staring at her.

"What?" She was bewildered by their dumbfounded expressions. Her plan was perfectly acceptable journalistic procedure.

"Nothing!" they said in unison. Owen scurried back into the print room, and Deanie Sue made busy at her desk.

When Ellin stepped out of the office late that afternoon, the sun was shining, and the temperature was well over forty degrees. Definitely pork-decomposing weather. She aimed the keyless entry device and unlocked her car door. Before she could get in, a familiar voice called out to her from across the street.

"Ellin! Wait up!"

Before turning around, she carefully fixed her expression to remove any sign that she was pleased to see him. She wouldn't give him the satisfaction of knowing she'd actually missed him this week. What was it about the spiky-haired English teacher that cranked up her heart rate and made her forget why she wanted to avoid him in the first place?

"Hello, Madden." Before he could reply, she added, "Sorry I can't hang around and chat, but I'm in a hurry."

"Really?" He seemed genuinely surprised. "What's urgent enough to warrant hurrying in Washington?"

"I'm working." She was momentarily distracted by his curious scent. A combination of chalk dust and—what? Lemons?

"Ah. Hot on the trail of a fast-breaking news story, are we?" He propped one gloved hand on the roof of the car and leaned against it.

"As a matter of fact." The way his shoulder strained the fabric of his overcoat reminded Ellin of the strength in his arms when he steadied her for the kiss under the mistletoe. It was a feeling she preferred not to remember.

"School's out for the day. Can I tag along? In an official capacity, of course."

"No need. As far as I know, sports are not even remotely involved." She couldn't tell him what *was* involved. She'd rather not let it get out that the award-winning investigative reporter, whose hard-hitting exposé had once uncovered the *legitimate* business dealings of a top Chicago crime lord, was on her way to interview a dead pig.

"I'm sorry I didn't call this week." He gave her a smile so warm it raised the ambient temperature several degrees.

She feigned indifference. "You didn't? I hadn't noticed."

"I got involved in my novel and lost track of time."

"What are you reading? It must be really good."

"I'm not reading a book," he clarified. "I'm writing one."

"Really?" Ellin folded her arms across her chest and leaned against the car's hood—a safe distance from the heat of his big wool-clad body. So he was a writer. Would this man ever stop surprising her?

"Really."

"How fascinating. What's it about?"

"Like many first novels, it's a bit autobiographical." His eyes twinkled behind his glasses. A clear challenge.

And one she couldn't resist. "So that would make it an in-depth character study that cuts to the very heart of the angst-ridden English-teaching profession?"

"Something like that."

"Can I read it sometime?" Perhaps doing so would give her insight into this puzzling man. And insight might provide a defense against him and his aggravating appeal.

"When it's ready to be read, you'll be the first to know."

"I'm a good editor," she pointed out. "With plenty of experience."

"I know you are."

"I could help you clean it up, get it ready to submit to a reputable publishing house. I know some literary agents, both in Chicago and New York. Why don't I phone and set something up? Better yet, I could call in some favors, maybe get a publisher to give it a read. You never know—"

"Whoa!" He grinned and jabbed his palm against his fingers in the universal time-out gesture. "I hate to be the one to have to remind you, but the position of managing editor puts you in charge the newspaper. It doesn't require you to run the rest of the world."

"I was just trying to help." The wind kicked up and ruffled his hair. Ellin had the sudden urge to reach up and smooth it back into place. Instead, she stuffed her hands in her pockets.

"I know you were. And I appreciate the offer. But I don't need editorial input just yet."

What he needed, she thought, was the input of a good, swift kick in the seat of his khakis. His sister was right. Jack Madden was not fulfilling his potential. And if someone did not shake up his complacent little world, he never would.

"So how long have you been working on The Great American Novel?"

"Four years, give or take." He shrugged. "What can I say? I have a fickle Muse."

"Hmm."

"I believe I detect distinct disapproval in that syllable."

"I think writers create their own inspiration. Using it, or its lack, as an excuse to avoid the risk of rejection is a form of self-delusion."

"Of course, being a risk-taker yourself, you would know all about such things."

He sounded sincere, but his earnestness irritated her. "If you don't take chances in life, you will never know what you're capable of accomplishing."

He nodded as though she'd just imparted the wisdom of the ages. "That's really profound. I think I found it in a fortune cookie once."

"I need to get going." God, the man was exasperating. He might be a nice guy and everybody's best friend, but he had no burning desire to get out of this safe little burg and make his mark on the world. Too bad. He had so much to offer. Wit and intelligence. Common sense. Artless integrity. And the kind of honesty that could not be faked.

Lack of self-confidence sure wasn't the problem. He was about as cocky as they came.

However, his contentment at being a big fish in a backwater pond was hard to understand. She believed success was what mattered most in the world and the way to achieve it was to work harder and smarter than everyone else. The best measure of success was the recognition it engendered, but Jack Madden didn't seem to require recognition outside his hometown.

She suspected that despite his many gifts, he lacked true ambition. That was one trait she found completely intolerable. And another excellent reason not to let him get too close.

"So where did you say you were off to again?" he asked with pointed interest.

"I don't believe I mentioned my destination."

"Oh, I remember. You're onto a big news story. Is it fodder for the front page, do you think?"

She winced. Jig Baker obviously thought so. "Maybe."

"Why don't I come over later and you can fix me dinner and tell me all about it."

She stared at him. Could he really have that much nerve, or was he just completely dense? "I don't think so."

"Okay," he said with boundless cheer. "You can come over to my house and I'll cook *you* dinner while you tell me all about it."

He obviously wasn't listening and had zero ability to read between the lines. She would just have to talk slowly and use little words. "No!"

"Want to go to Mama Maria's for a pizza later? It's buy-one-get-one-for-half-price night."

"No, I don't want any pizza. I am not going out with you, Madden."

"We don't have to go out. In fact, I prefer to stay in. It's much cozier that way."

"You don't get it, do you? Nothing's going to happen between us. Haven't I made myself clear on that point? If not, I can take out a full-page ad in the *Post-Ette*. Or have it painted on the side of a barn. Maybe I could hire a sky-writer to scrawl it across the heavens in really tall letters. Would that help?"

"Nah, that won't be necessary," he said with a good-natured shrug. "I can take a hint."

"Is that right? Because so far you've given no indication that you possess any such ability." She had to get away from this guy before she totally lost it. And agreed to one of his crazy, cozy dinner options.

He smiled. "I should let you get back on the trail of that titillating news story. I'd feel just terrible if our biggest competitor, *The Pine Valley Voice*, scooped you on it."

She rolled her eyes before getting in the car and starting the engine. He tapped on the window, and she punched the button, allowing the side window to slide down soundlessly between them. "Yes, Madden? What is it now?"

"Just a friendly warning. Don't go *hog*-wild with that story now."

Jack chuckled as he watched her drive off in a cloud of indignant exhaust vapor. Winning over Ellin Bennett was turning out to be just about the most fun he'd ever had. He did not doubt the outcome, but he was sure enjoying the process. He'd always loved a challenge. Just thinking the "L" word filled him with a sense of fateful joy. Love. Yeah, it could definitely happen.

Ellin still didn't know how inevitable it was. Or how determined he could be. When he dangled the bait, she jumped at it like a hungry trout, but she still gamely resisted being reeled in. No problem. He had more than one lure in his tackle box.

He never knew a woman's confused frustration could be so adorable. Or so damned sexy. Maybe it was because he knew it was a whole new state of being for her, and he'd caused it. Despite his protests to the contrary, it had taken every bit of his self-control earlier not to grab her like a caveman and cover that bossy little face of hers with damp kisses. But that's what she expected him to do. She was geared up for a frontal assault and would have pulled out the heavy artillery.

Clearly, she was used to dealing with Type-A men who didn't have time for covert tactics or guerrilla romance. Jana and her infernal mistletoe had forced him into making an ill-advised move Christmas Day. Not that he hadn't thoroughly enjoyed the kiss. It just wasn't the time or place for it. Like any good strategist he had retreated long enough to develop a new plan. Now he was ready for action. She didn't realize it yet, but Ellin Bennett didn't stand a chance. He was going to wear down her defenses and show her how good they could be together.

His parents had given him their blessing when he told them Ellin was "The One" and he planned to actively pursue her. They respected his decision because they had always assured him he'd "know" when he met the right woman. They liked Ellin and were utterly charmed by her little girl.

His mother's only concern was that three months didn't seem like much time to conduct a meaningful courtship. But his father had reminded her that while their courtship had only lasted two-and-one-half months, their marriage had survived thirty-five years.

All and all, Jack felt pretty good about himself, the future and his chances to win the woman of his dreams. In fact, he felt too good. It was time to head over to Jana's office for a little reality therapy. No one could put things into perspective better than his twin.

"Well, if it isn't Casanova of the Ozarks." Jana looked up at him from a client's tax return and grinned. "What's new on the romance front?"

"Ellin just refused to have dinner with me and drove off in a petulant huff." He sat in his accustomed chair and stretched out his legs.

"So, you're making progress then." She leaned back in her chair. "I hate to burst your bubble, but—"

"No, you don't. It's what you live for."

She seemed to think it over. "That's true. Let's see, you have roughly twelve weeks before the exalted Ms. Bennett moves on to bigger and better things. Do you think she'll actually accept a date with you before she goes?"

"She's not going to leave."

"Well, to hear her tell it, she is."

"Don't fret yourself, she'll change her mind."

She smiled sweetly. "It must be such a comfort to live in your own little world where bad things like facts and reality can't intrude upon your delusions of grandeur."

He gave himself a mock slap on the cheek. "Thanks, I needed that."

Jana's smile faded and she focused on him with genuine concern. "I can make fun of you, Jack, but you know I'd fight anyone else who did."

"I still haven't gotten over the humiliation of you punching Karen Lee Holstead on my behalf in the third grade."

She flexed her biceps. "Do you think I could take Ellin Bennett?"

"Hopefully it won't come to that. She's putting up a good fight, but I have a plan."

"Oh, boy. That's a scary thought." She leaned forward,

her expression suddenly serious. "I don't want to see you get hurt."

"Good. We agree on something."

"I'm afraid you might be taking this a little more seriously than you should. I like Ellin. She's a smart lady. But she's a 24/7 kind of go-getter. Beyond ambitious. I really don't see her being content to settle down in Washington, Arkansas. She told me she was planning to apply for a position with a big-city paper."

"I know."

"And that doesn't impact on your little plans?"

"Right now, she thinks she's leaving. But I'm still in phase one. She'll change her mind."

"And if she doesn't?"

"Don't worry, she will. I have a strategy. Twelve weeks is plenty of time to convince her how lovable I am. You'll see."

Jack wouldn't even consider the possibility of rejection. He'd made up his mind. She was "The One." He would show her that he was "The One" for her, too. The emotions he felt when he was with her were too powerful to be one-sided. She had to feel them. She just wasn't as open to the possibilities as he was.

Yet.

# Chapter Six

Composing, printing and distributing the weekly *Post-Ette* was not nearly so complicated an operation as putting a big-city daily to bed. However, Ellin was no less relieved when the tedious process was finally completed. By Friday afternoon she was filled with an unexpected sense of accomplishment and optimism. She located a brand new binder, labeled it with the new year and ceremoniously filed away Wednesday's edition for posterity.

One down, eleven to go.

She high-fived Owen who nodded and blushed every shade on the red end of the spectrum. "Great going, people. All in all, not a bad little newspaper, even without the infamous hog story. Thanks again for your help."

Deanie Sue dropped the day's deposit into the bank bag and closed it with a quick zip. "You done good, El. We got four ads, two new subscriptions and three renewals out of that issue."

Ellin smiled. Forget the Pulitzer. What greater glory could a journalist hope for than to increase sales and earn a Deanie Sue-bestowed nickname? Circulation success wasn't measured in the thousands here, she reminded herself. Four ads, two subscriptions and three renewals in one week *were* a big deal.

Once the case of the decaying porker was closed and the story reduced to a one-inch column on page three, Ellin had realized there was a big blank space on the front page. In a rush to find something newsworthy enough to fill it, she'd ended up covering behind-the-scene preparations for one of the volunteer fire department's frequent fund raisers.

What started out as fluff and filler developed into a human interest story detailing the selfless efforts of local volunteers and their desperate need for updated fire fighting equipment. She raided Jig's old photo files in order to feature the grim, sooty faces of firemen alongside shots of their 1967 model fire truck. She described the lime green secondhand beauty they hoped to acquire and the rescue equipment they needed to save the lives of accident victims. Her report had generated favorable comments from subscribers and renewed public interest in the department's goal of raising an additional $40,000.

"I'm going to get Lizzie," Ellin told Deanie Sue and Owen as she slipped into her coat. "I'll see you both later at the chili supper."

"You'd better get there early," the bookkeeper advised. "I hear they're expecting a good showing because of your story. They might run out."

"I don't think so," Owen put in. "Annie Jenkins over at the Sav-A-Lot said they're cooking up the biggest batch of chili ever. She said they have enough to feed Lee's army."

And it was a good thing they did. At the end of the evening when the auxiliary ladies were dishing up the last of the spicy concoction, Mary Madden told Ellin that her consciousness-raising article had resulted in the biggest chili supper turnout in recent memory, as well as record contributions to the equipment fund.

And it was all because of her. Ellin couldn't stop smiling. She really had "done good." In Chicago it was difficult to know if her dedication and hard work really made a difference in the lives of others. Not so in Washington. The positive feedback was up-close and immediate. Fire Chief Hal Madden had taken her aside and personally thanked her for the story. It had brought in people from two counties. Never before had so many been so willing to risk heartburn for a good cause.

She was still glowing from his grateful praise and helping Jana wipe tables when Jack came over. She'd been surprised to learn he was a member of the volunteer fire crew but should have expected as much. Was there anything he *didn't* do? He shot his sister a look that sent her scurrying elsewhere for something to do.

Ellin feigned attention while he talked and tried not to notice what a fine masculine figure he cut in his bulky green sweater, pressed jeans and waffle-soled boots. Unfortunately, he was a hard man to ignore.

"Everyone's talking about how you called the head of the State Health Department," he said.

"Calling was easy. Convincing her that a decomposing animal carcass posed a serious threat to public health and hygiene was the hard part."

"But you did it."

She dismissed that with a nod. The director had eventually concurred with her assessment and sent out a disposal crew.

Jack grinned and gave her a thumbs-up gesture. "Hog gone. Stalemate over. Political tinderbox effectively defused. End of story. You're amazing."

Ellin couldn't risk clinging to the compliment or falling into the daring depths of his dark eyes. So she scrubbed at a spot on the vinyl tablecloth and modestly proclaimed she'd only done what any other concerned citizen would have done.

"Maybe," he said. "Only no one else did *anything*. Except point fingers and pass the buck."

"I guess they just hadn't thought of the obvious yet."

"But you did. You saw through the smoke and went straight for the solution. People can't stop talking about it. They've just about decided maybe you aren't as stuck-up as they thought."

"That's a relief. Now I can sleep at night."

"You showed them what can be done and how to do it. Maybe they won't be so quick to dodge the next bullet that comes their way."

"Just call me Lois Lane, Girl Crusader." His respect meant a lot to her, but she didn't want him to know how much. Flippancy was always a good cover. Since there was no way to avoid him in a town this small, the next few months would go much more smoothly if she could just keep the friendly antagonism alive. At least on the surface.

He leaned against the edge of the table and she caught another subtle whiff of his citrusy cologne. At least she thought it was cologne. Maybe he washed his clothes in lemon-fresh detergent. Or perhaps he was a closet lemonade abuser. He didn't seem to have any other vices or bad habits.

"I don't think you realize how much things have changed since you arrived. Or how much more they *will* change." He took the dishcloth out of her hand and replaced it with one of the two disposable cups of iced tea he'd brought with him.

"Here's to change."

She had no choice but to join him in the impromptu toast. "To change." She was all too aware of the intense look he focused on her, his head cocked slightly to capture her reluctant gaze. There had been nothing suggestive in his words, so why did she suspect they possessed a meaning she did not understand? And why did a rush of heat as hot as a welder's torch suddenly sweep through her body?

She tried to sip the cold drink to douse the fire, but she'd mysteriously lost the ability to swallow. The room tilted like a fun house floor. For a bare flash of a moment she almost forgot they were in a public place among other people, including impressionable young children. She wanted nothing more than to slip her hands under that fuzzy sweater, find his warm, hard flesh and...

Ellin froze, shocked by the unbidden and lascivious thought of exactly what it was she wanted to do to Jack Madden. Whoa. Something very spooky was going on here. She'd never been the carnal type, but if that last impulse was not based on pure animal lust, she was even more confused than she thought. What was wrong with her? She was not a hormonal high schooler. She was almost thirty-five years old. She had long since perfected self-control *and* self-denial. Feelings like this were annoying distractions that bogged her down and interfered with her focus.

She'd worked professionally with plenty of men over the years. Brilliant, talented men. Socially, she'd had her fair share of promising dates and near-miss relationships. But none of them, not even her ex-husband, had inspired the overwhelming desire for physical possession she felt right now.

No. She wouldn't even consider going there. Having the hots for the local English teacher was not a viable option. Three months from now she'd be gone. And wondering what the heck she'd been thinking. She liked Jack too much to engage in a torrid affair that relegated him to status of permanent regret.

She was a mother, for God's sake. And in serious danger of totally losing her credibility.

With uncanny perceptiveness, he seemed to understand exactly what was happening. He leaned in close, whispering so no one else could hear. His voice was soft, his breath warm and fruity on her cheek. It calmed her fluttering heart.

"You know, Ellin, if you toss a pebble into the ocean it will sink forever without ever making a ripple. But if you throw that same pebble into a small pond it will create waves that eventually wash ashore and touch all who walk there."

Holy-moley. She had to get out of here. Surely he didn't expect her to hang around and drink tea after dropping that little philosophical bomb on her. She was so mixed-up, the guy was actually beginning to make sense. Shoving her troublesome needs aside, she turned away from him without a word, located Lizzie, grabbed their coats and escaped into the night.

Jana walked over and leaned against the table beside him, a frown on her face. "Jack?"

"Yeah?"

"That didn't go too well."

"Oh, you're wrong." He smiled. Ellin had tried to hide it, but there was no concealing the blaze of desire in her eyes. "As a matter of fact, that went unbelievably well." He wouldn't tell his sister that for a moment there he'd been in serious danger of being pushed back on the table and ravished in front of God and everybody. Or that a cold shower loomed in his immediate future.

"You're down to eleven weeks, you know."

"I know."

"That's not much time."

"'Oh, ye of little faith.' Clearly, you underestimate my power to charm and influence women."

"Maybe. I have seen you in action, after all." She punched him playfully on the arm. "You may be a brilliant writer, but your math is not what it should be, genius. I'm afraid you might have *overestimated* said power."

For the next couple of weeks, Ellin didn't have to worry about finding stories to fill the *Post-Ette*'s eight pages. Area high schools were in competition for a slot in the Class AA basketball playoffs. The town's sports-crazed inhabitants were far more interested in whether or not the Warriors had a shot at the state championship than in the strife occurring elsewhere in the world.

Jack was in and out of the office almost every day in his capacity as sports reporter. Ellin had built a career based on attention to detail, but no one could ever accuse Jack Madden of sweating the small stuff. His laid-back ideology of "work to live" was the antithesis of her "live to work" ethos, and his laissez-faire attitude toward things like professional form and deadlines was a constant irritation. Whenever their differences dissolved into name calling, he declared her habits obsessive, she proclaimed his slipshod.

One day he stood by her desk, fumbling around in his backpack for the player profiles that were scheduled to run in the next day's edition.

"You know, those were supposed to be turned in yesterday," she reprimanded him. "Owen is waiting for them."

"I know. Hang on a minute. I have them here somewhere."

"Do you even own a briefcase?" she asked in exasperation.

He held up the worn leather knapsack. "Don't need

one." When he couldn't find what he was looking for, he shrugged. "Oh, well. I must have left them at school. Tell Owen to go ahead without them. You can come up with some dazzling filler and we'll run the profiles next week."

"Give me that." She snatched the pack to make a methodical search. She didn't have time to write filler, dazzling or otherwise. She began removing items which she laid in a neat row on her desk. A clutch of ungraded student essays. Highlighter pens. An aging banana. A paperback copy of Poe's collected works. A half-eaten bag of lemon drops.

"I think I've figured out what your official motto should be," she told him in frustration.

"What?" His interest seemed sincere.

"I'm not sure of the Latin, but it goes something like, 'When unable to postpone, blow it off.'"

He nodded in agreement. "I like it. Could you work that up in needlepoint for my office? In the school colors?"

"You're hopeless. Ha!" She produced the missing article and smoothed the crumpled paper on her desk.

"No, I'm very hopeful. In fact, I'm a veritable fount of hope. Want to know your motto?"

She knew she'd regret it, but couldn't resist that teasing look. "Why not?"

"If something is worth doing, it's worth doing yourself."

"There's nothing wrong with wanting to be in control," she defended. "Life is too serious to be taken so lightly."

"That's where you're wrong, boss." He stuffed his gear back into his backpack and slung it over his shoulder. "Life is too short to be taken so seriously."

He paused at the door. "There's another game tonight over in Hilldale. Do you want to share a box of popcorn and cuddle on the bleachers with me?"

"As tempting as you make it sound, no thanks." How

many times did she have to turn him down? Either the man was as dense as a box of rocks or he had a bullet-proof ego. He seemed to thrive on rejection.

"Maybe I'll stop by the house before the game. Just to say hi to Ida Faye."

"There's no law against visiting shut-ins." She was already editing his copy.

He laughed, and she threw a pencil at him as he ducked out the door.

He was impossible. And it was equally impossible not to like him. She just couldn't afford to cross the line and allow liking to become something more. Maintaining her defenses against him was second nature now. But given his persistence level, each encounter became a test of her endurance.

He'd been by the house several times since Ida Faye's discharge from the nursing home. He never showed up without a roll of the old lady's favorite butterscotch-flavored candy, and a small treat or trinket for Lizzie. He even carried dog biscuits for Pudgy. He was cordial to Ellin, but never overly attentive, which was the way she wanted it. Still, for some unexamined reason it bugged her that she was the only member of the household who didn't benefit from his generosity. Not that she'd ever let him know that.

She hated to admit it, but Lizzie and Ida Faye weren't the only ones who'd come to look forward to his visits.

Lizzie had gotten new shoes and had promptly decorated the box with stickers and glitter, turning it into a "treasure chest" to hold the things Jack gave her. Ellin often found her poring over her booty. A shiny piece of fool's gold. A cardinal's red feather. An Indian Head penny. A miniature storybook he found in a cereal box. Santa's magic key which she was saving for next year.

Ellin suspected her daughter valued the giver more than the gifts and worried that she was getting too attached. Lizzie tagged after Jack like a lonesome puppy while he made small repairs around the house. She hung on his every word as he explained the crucial difference between a regular screwdriver and a Phillips, and told her how the monkey wrench got its name. She listened attentively as he read her stories, and she often saved new books to share with him first.

Ellin suspected Lizzie's fondness for the only man in her life was growing into hero worship. She knew for certain when her little girl asked him to repair the ripped seam in her favorite stuffed dog.

"I can sew that for you, princess," she'd told her.

"I want Jack to do it," she'd declared. "Santa gave me this doggy, and Jack is Santa's friend."

Jack not only stitched up the rip, he let Lizzie thread the needle. When he was done, he borrowed a heart-shaped button from Ida Faye's button jar and sewed it on the pup's chest. That simple, whimsical act delighted Lizzie but made Ellin feel like the world's worst mommy. She never would have thought of giving the pup a heart.

Lizzie was not only getting attached to Jack, but to Jana's children Colton and Laurel, with whom she played. She adored her sitter, Mrs. Kendall, and was always reluctant to leave at the end of the day, even when Ellin assured her she could come back tomorrow. When the time came, her daughter would have a hard time breaking those ties.

The only attachment Ellin wasn't worried about was the one Lizzie had formed with Ida Faye. The elderly lady wasn't yet nimble enough to care for the active four-year-old all day, but they spent a lot of time together. Lizzie loved looking through Ida Faye's old photo albums and was fascinated by a picture of a curly-haired preschooler who bore a striking resemblance to her. She begged for the picture of her mother to put in her treasure box.

Ellin had always regretted that her parents' acrimonious divorce had cheated her out of time with her father and grandmother. She blamed her mother for the childhood loss but had no excuse for the last twenty years. As an adult, she should have made time to strengthen the bond with her family. She always planned to but had been so involved in the hectic minutiae of her own life, she'd permanently postponed her visits.

Until it was too late. She couldn't go back and retrieve what she'd thrown away. She knew that now. When Ida Faye came home from the nursing center she removed a box from under her bed. Inside was a thick stack of envelopes tied with a blue ribbon. The old lady had found them among her son's things after his death from colon cancer and wanted Ellin to have them.

Ellin had opened the envelopes later that night, long after Ida Faye and Lizzie had fallen into their dreams.

Ed Boswell had saved every greeting card his daughter had ever sent him. Father's Day. Christmas. Birthdays. Just to Say Hello. Across the Miles. She recognized some of colorful illustrations and recalled how she'd grabbed them off a store display, scrawled a hurried sentiment inside, and mailed them on her way to somewhere else. It was the hollow promises they contained that squeezed her heart and made her realize how much she'd given up.

*Sorry I can't be with you on your special day. Maybe next year,* read one. *Missing you this holiday season,* she'd written in another. *Hope your birthday is happy. Sorry you're under the weather. Get well soon. I'm thinking of you.*

But who had she really been thinking of? At the time, she'd meant what she said. But words were never enough.

Her Dad never told her about the cancer, and Ida Faye said he hadn't wanted her to worry. But that didn't excuse her selfishness. She should have been here for him. She could never make it up, but just seeing Lizzie's blond head bent close to Ida Faye's white one over the family album went a long way toward assuaging the pain of remorse.

That night she had placed the cards in the drawer of her nightstand, and there they remained. A guilt-edged reminder of opportunity missed.

There was no way to regain the years she'd lost with her father, but she could be with her grandmother, at least for the next few weeks. And later, she would make good on those empty promises she'd made. She would come back. It wouldn't be fair to do otherwise. Her grandmother took special joy in sharing stories of her own girlhood with Lizzie, in rolling out cookie dough for her clumsy little fingers to cut, and in teaching her how to make hot chocolate from scratch.

Ellin was glad circumstances, or fate, had knocked her off the self-absorbed ladder she'd been climbing so long. It had led her to this quiet little town in the mountains, so far from the world she knew. She'd thought she could breeze in here and show the yokels a thing or two about running a newspaper.

Instead she was the one who was learning. Jack Madden was the tender teacher who taught her there was more than one way to live. In doing so, his life was gradually becoming entwined with hers. Even her grandmother had noticed. During one of their talks, she cautioned Ellin to "be nice to that boy and don't go toying with his feelings."

She'd silenced Ellin's protests by describing a morning glory vine that had steadily wound its way up a shrub in her backyard last summer. She said it was a pretty sight when the blue flowers opened to the sun. But she knew it would last only one season, while the spirea had been there for years. If she had allowed the morning glory to flourish unchecked, eventually the two could not have been separated. The weight of the vine would have uprooted the bush and destroyed it. So she'd chosen to sacrifice the temporary beauty of one plant for the permanent reliability of the other.

Ellin didn't think her grandmother really meant to compare her to a strangling vine, but the message was clear. She was beginning to understand just how deep Jack's roots went in the community. Washington was his whole world. As much as she enjoyed her time here, she had a life outside its comfortable cocoon. Come the end of March, she would definitely move on.

And Jack would stay. She might not understand him, but she knew him well enough to suspect nothing could induce him to leave his home. Which meant she had to double her efforts to rebuff him. She had plans. Long-standing goals. And a young daughter to provide for. If she had to harden her hungry heart to keep her priorities in focus, that's what she would do. She had to forget about feelings and think only of her future. And Lizzie's.

She was a single mother and she wanted her daughter to have advantages and opportunities in life. But advantages cost money. She had to think ahead, go where the money was. And opportunities? There wouldn't be many of those in Washington.

So no matter how charming and appealing Jack might be, she had to keep the twining tendrils of his life completely separate from her own. It was the only way either of them could escape damage.

## *Chapter Seven*

"It ain't like Jack to forget to turn in his copy." Owen had finished most of the layouts for the latest edition of the *Post-Ette*. He'd been waiting all day for the report on last night's championship basketball game. "We gotta run something. This is the first time in eight years the Wildcats have made it to the state finals."

The fact that the team had lost by three points and ended up placing second in the tournament apparently didn't diminish the event's importance. Ellin glanced at the clock in aggravation. Not that it mattered. Jack didn't even wear a watch. He seemed to operate by some internal Madden Standard Time, which was completely out of synch with any of the known time zones of the world.

But why did he have to be so late today of all days? She was in no mood for his games. Lizzie had awakened her at 6:00 a.m. by crawling into her bed and promptly throwing up. You'd think that if you got puked on first thing in the morning, nothing worse could happen to you all day. But no. Things had definitely gone downhill from there.

She'd comforted her feverish daughter, given her a baby aspirin to bring down her temperature, cleaned up the mess and stuffed the soiled bedding into the washing machine. Which then backed up and drained soapy water all over the utility room floor. Ida Faye had promised to call in someone to fix it, and insisted she could deal with Lizzie's ailment which was probably just a twenty-four-hour virus. That didn't keep Ellin from being distracted with worry. Back in Chicago, she'd used her own sick days to stay home when Lizzie was too ill to go to day care, but that wasn't an option today.

When she got ready to leave for work, she couldn't locate her key ring. After a protracted search of the house, she found it in Lizzie's treasure box tucked alongside the pretty cardinal feather. Her attempt to make up for lost time only netted her a speeding ticket. She had recklessly tempted fate on Main Street by doing twenty-eight miles per hour in a twenty-five-mile-per-hour zone. At least her wanton criminal activities had given Leland the Cop something to do.

By the time she got to the office, she was beyond late and in serious need of a caffeine fix. She headed straight for the coffee machine, checking her inbox en route. Both were as empty as a baby's conscience. She made a fresh pot and hastily cleared the evidence of Owen's late-night snack off her desk. She'd finally settled down to work, but was forced to slurp java all day just to keep up the momentum.

Now it was after four o'clock, and dangerously close to the Tuesday afternoon cutoff. She couldn't wait much longer, she wanted to get home and check on Lizzie. If they did not get the final pages laid out soon, the paper would not be ready for distribution tomorrow. And that was not going to happen. Ellin Bennett did not miss deadlines.

If she couldn't get a small potatoes eight-page newspaper out on time, she would just get out of journalism and take up underwater basket weaving.

"What do you think we oughta do?" Owen asked, still waiting.

"Let me try to reach Jack one more time." She'd already left two messages. Which he had not deigned to return. She dialed the high school and was told he was in play practice and would be tied up until eight.

Dammit! They couldn't wait that long. Ellin felt that old familiar stress reaction creeping up on her. She'd dealt with it daily in Chicago, but it had been pleasantly absent since her arrival in Washington. She wrestled it for control and made an editorial decision. After getting the final score and a few key highlights from the secretary, she turned to the computer keyboard and typed a brief no-nonsense report of the game. She handed the sheet to Owen when it came out of the printer.

"That's it?" he asked with obvious misgivings.

"It'll have to do." Damn Jack anyway for putting her in this position. His indifference to deadlines indicated a lack of professionalism that had finally crossed the line from mild irritant to major problem.

Was it possible to fire a volunteer correspondent?

"Run the long version of Mabel Howard's hundredth birthday party story. The one her granddaughter turned in. That should take up the slack."

"You're the boss." Owen headed for the workroom.

Ellin forced her thoughts away from Jack's inconsiderate behavior before she became even angrier. She called home, and Ida Faye told her Lizzie was feeling much better. She'd kept down some soup and a couple of the ice pops Ellin had taken her at lunchtime. She was propped up on the couch watching cartoons, wearing her princess crown and surrounded by pillows and stuffed animals. Her grand-mother assured her things were fine and to stop worrying.

Ellin tried but didn't quite succeed. She took motherhood very seriously. Having children had never been part of her grand plan since she'd always assumed she wasn't really mommy material. Then she'd had Lizzie and all that had changed. There were still moments when she doubted her qualifications, but she could no longer imagine her life without the little princess.

Andrew had not been pleased when she'd gotten preg-nant during their first year of marriage. He had accused her of being careless. As if conception were a do-it-yourself project. The doctor had speculated that she'd most likely hit the ovum lottery following a bout of the flu during which she'd been unable to keep anything down. Including her birth control pills.

Andrew had finally come around to a level of acceptance, but he was an even more career-minded journalist than Ellin. He'd jumped at the chance to go to Lebanon as an interim bureau chief when Lizzie was only six months old. He hadn't returned to the states until she was nearly two. By that time, the marriage was over, and it had been a simple matter to tie up the legal loose ends.

They had been too busy and self-absorbed to engage in the bitter fighting that had characterized her parents' union. They couldn't point fingers or cast blame because neither of them had really tried to make it work. They'd simply been too involved in their professions, always competing for the next rung on the career ladder. Their marriage had been based on lukewarm sex and one-upmanship, so their divorce had been rather anticlimactic.

However, that hadn't made it any less painful.

Lizzie was completely recovered by the next day. Ellin dropped her off with the sitter who told her the McGovern children had also been sick the day before. Apparently, bugs spread quickly among preschoolers.

As it turned out, reader dissatisfaction was just as virulent among the paper's subscribers. Especially those with sons on the basketball team. Or anyone who knew someone with a son on the team. Which pretty much covered everybody in town.

When Ellin got to the office, Owen informed her that Deanie Sue had already fielded a number of complaints about the game report they had printed in the paper. The older woman hung up after another call as Ellin poured her first cup of coffee.

"Lay it on me," Ellin said grimly, expecting the worst.

"Well, that was Tim Jackson's mama," she said. "She was none too happy that we didn't mention the sixteen points her baby boy made in Monday night's game."

Ellin took a big sip of the hot brew. "What did you tell her?"

"The same thing I've told everybody else who's called. That I'm just the office manager and don't have anything to do with content. I said she'd have to talk to the editor, and she said she'd be getting back to you. That's about the same thing Lloyd Davis's mama said, and Pete Johnson's daddy, and Mike Mueller's Uncle Phil."

"Oh, great."

"And a couple of the cheerleaders are mad 'cause we didn't brag on their new routine."

"The next time someone calls, tell them I was abducted by space aliens during a crop circle incident last night."

"But there aren't any crops now. It's winter."

"That was a joke, Deanie Sue."

"Oh. Right. Good one, El." The bookkeeper pulled out her ledgers and did whatever it was she did to them.

Ellin leaned back in her chair and stretched to ease her aching muscles. This time she'd tossed a pebble into the pond and it had ricocheted back to conk her on the noggin. Damn Jack Madden anyway. This was all his fault. If he'd taken his responsibility seriously, instead of blowing it off in favor of something more fun, she wouldn't be strapped in the hot seat. She planned to give him a very large piece of her mind the next time his spiky little head darkened her door.

She didn't have long to wait. At ten o'clock, which was his planning period at school, he sauntered in waving a copy of the *Post-Ette*. "What the heck happened to my story?"

"Good question, Madden. And one I'd like to have answered. As would half the rabid sports fans in Washington."

"What are you talking about?" He shucked out of his coat and dropped it on the counter.

"Didn't you get my messages yesterday?"

"No, I did not get any messages." He seemed to remember something and grimaced. "Uh-oh. I may not have checked my box."

"Well, we checked ours. In fact, we waited until nearly five o'clock for you to turn in your copy." She was steamed, and it did not matter one bit how good he looked in his hunter-green pinwale corduroy shirt and knife-creased khakis. He had tarnished her reputation, and he would pay.

"I left it on your desk on my way to school yesterday. I had an early faculty meeting, so I didn't have time to put it in the computer, but it was all written out."

"Don't give me that. I looked for it. My inbox was empty."

Jack didn't understand what was going on, but there was

no mistaking the censure in Ellin's voice or the fire in her eyes. Both hurt more than he'd thought possible. This time her barely controlled anger was sorely misdirected because he was innocent of the crime for which he stood accused. But in Ellin's opinion, he was obviously guilty until he could prove otherwise.

Clearly, words would not be enough to placate her. He scattered the compulsively neat stacks of papers on her desk, looking for evidence. When he didn't find what he was searching for, he started in on the wastepaper basket. That's when Deanie Sue shoved away from her desk and joined Owen in the work room to avoid being caught in the crossfire.

"What are you doing?" Ellin demanded. "Do you think I'd throw away your stupid story just to get myself in trouble with team moms and cheerleaders?"

"No. But I do think your obsessive orderliness is at fault here. Not me."

"Yeah, right." She made a frank body language statement by clamping her arms across her chest.

Her eyes widened in surprise when he overturned the trash can and produced the document in question. With a triumphant "Aha!" he held up the flattened popcorn box he had carefully torn open at the seam. The back was covered with his best teacher penmanship.

"What the heck is that?" she asked as he slapped it down in front of her.

"My basketball story. I told you I left it on your desk. You threw it in the trash."

"You wrote it on a popcorn box?" she asked incredulously, her volume increasing with her disbelief. "A popcorn box? I know you don't feel the constraint of professionalism, but what kind of reporter writes an important story on a freaking popcorn box?"

"A kid spilled his soft drink on my notebook. It was the only paper I had. It may be a little salty, but it is perfectly legible."

"I thought Owen had been eating at my desk again," she said. "It never occurred to me to look on the back."

"Because you preferred to believe I'm such a slacker that I would let you down?" He studied her face. Several emotions flitted across her features before she settled on defeat.

"I'm sorry." At least she made a stab at sincerity. "I guess I should have known you wouldn't leave us flapping in the wind. But a popcorn box? Really, Madden."

"It was handy. I wanted to get the story down while it was happening. To capture all the excitement along with the crowd's reactions."

She read over the lost article. When she finished, she looked up with an apologetic smile. "It's good. It would have made much better copy than Mabel Howard's birthday party. You even commended the cheerleaders."

"Hey, they had a new cheer. And Kristy Evans finally managed to do a double back flip without falling on her can."

Ellin covered her face with her hands. "Jeez, everyone in town hates me now."

"It's all right. You can blame me. Just tell them what happened."

She rolled her eyes. "Blame you? Yeah, right. And put a black mark on your sterling character? I don't think so. I'd rather face an angry lynch mob."

He pulled a chair close to hers and sat down. Then he took her hand in his, surprised that she allowed the contact. "You can trust me, Ellin. You have to believe I would never do anything to upset or disappoint you. I wouldn't dream of putting you in a bad light. That just isn't my style.''

"Okay.'' She tried to wiggle her hand free, but he wasn't quite ready to let go.

"When I didn't answer your messages yesterday, why didn't you come to the school and look for me? Or send Owen? Or ask the secretary to dispatch a student runner to find me?''

"It never occurred to me. It was your responsibility to turn in the story. I guess I thought—''

"That I'd blown it off?''

"Something like that.''

He tipped her chin up with his thumb and forced her to meet his gaze. "Jumping to conclusions is not the best form of aerobic exercise, you know.''

"Ah, poopers! People are really mad at me.''

Poopers? "And you care?''

"Well, of course I care. I liked it better when everyone thought I was the Goddess of Journalism.''

"If it's any consolation, I still think you are.''

She slipped her hand from his and picked up a pointy pencil to fend off any further advances he might make. "Do you think the villagers are out gathering up their pitchforks, even as we speak?''

He shook his head. "I doubt it. We Arkansans prefer tar and feathers.''

The depth of her sigh told him exactly how tired she was. He moved behind her chair and kneaded the tense muscles in her shoulders.

"Whatever it is you think you're doing, just stop it!'' Her words would have carried more weight if her tone hadn't been so darned squeaky.

"I'm just working out some of your kinks. Try to relax. Your muscles are knottier than a macramé wall hanging.''

She tried to fight him, but persistence paid off as he felt the tightness slowly dissolve under his fingers.

"You have no business touching my muscles, Madden. I don't care how knotty they are."

It wasn't a very convincing protest, he thought. Especially in light of the way her head dropped forward to expose the slender column of her neck. But it was all those pining little sighs that were his undoing. His flesh quickened, and his body overheated when he thought of other, more interesting ways to elicit her moans of pleasure.

He imagined how warm her skin would feel beneath his hands, how soft her body would feel beneath his. He could almost taste her sweet mouth as he breathed in the flower scent of her hair. He had to put a hasty end to the massage before he weakened and did something rash that would undo what little progress he'd managed to make. He stepped away from her before she completely overwhelmed his senses.

"As much as I'd like to heap this on your head, Jack, I'm big enough to accept responsibility." She avoided looking at him by straightening the papers on her desk. "Since you're the Jedi master of shmooze, do you have any suggestions on how I can get myself out of this mess?"

He grinned, relieved that the misunderstanding about the story hadn't compromised their fledgling relationship. If he'd had any niggling suspicion that he might be barking up the wrong romantic tree, it had vanished. He'd felt Ellin melt under his touch. If a shoulder massage could evoke that kind of response, wait until she got the full sensual effect of some serious foreplay.

"That's easy," he told her. "All you have to do is let people know the story was omitted due to an oversight. They'll understand because, being humans themselves, they know everyone makes mistakes. Even journalism goddesses. Then just run the story next week.''

''But it'll be old news by then,'' she protested.

''Maybe in the universal scheme of things. But the mamas and the cheerleaders will have the newspaper clipping for their scrapbooks and everyone will be happy.''

''And my journalistic honor will be restored?''

''It was never in question.''

''Why did you set four places at the table?'' Ellin asked her grandmother when she arrived home later that evening. The little house was filled with the delicious smells of home cooking. ''Are you expecting a guest for dinner?''

''Matter of fact, I am.'' Leaning on her quad-cane, Ida Faye pulled an open roasting pan out of the oven and basted a plump chicken that was slowly turning brown.

Ellin peeked into the covered pans on the stove. Potatoes in parsley butter and green beans. ''Yum. Smells good.''

''Who's coming, Grammy?'' Lizzie jumped up and down. ''Is it Jack? I hope it's Jack. Say it's Jack.''

Ellin's breath caught. *Please, don't say it's Jack.* The memory of his touch and how she'd responded to it this afternoon would make it difficult, if not impossible, to sit across the table from him and eat chicken.

''Why, yes, Princess Liz. It *is* Jack.'' Ida Faye placed packaged rolls on a baking sheet. ''He's going to take a look at that dang washing machine for me. The least I can do is fix him a good supper. Don't you imagine single fellas get tired of batching it all the time?''

''Oh, goody!'' Lizzie clapped her hands in excitement. ''I'm gonna pick out some books. I bet he'll want to read me a story.''

''He's coming to fix the washer, princess. He probably

won't have time to hang around when he's done.'' At least Ellin hoped he wouldn't.

Ida Faye gave her a speculative look and wiped her hands on her apron. ''Oh, I think he will. He said he didn't have anything else going on tonight.''

''Oh, goody,'' Ellin muttered.

''He'll be here in a few minutes,'' her grandmother said. ''But you still have time to freshen up and change out of that suit.''

Ellin smoothed her navy blue skirt. ''What's wrong with it?''

''Nothing if you're headed to a board meeting. Why don't you put on something more suitable for entertaining a gentleman caller?''

''Jack Madden is *not* my gentleman caller,'' she protested.

''Didn't say he was.'' Ida Faye gave Lizzie a playful wink. ''But he's ours, ain't he, princess?''

''Yep,'' Lizzie agreed with a giggle. She turned to her mother and pushed her out of the kitchen. ''Wear your fluffy shirt, Mommy. It's pretty.''

Half an hour later, Ellin sat at the table across from Jack, picking at her food and feeling extremely uncomfortable in her ''fluffy'' shirt, a silky lavender number that dripped ruffles down the front and from the sleeves. She'd worn it with designer jeans and dangling silver earrings, but wished now that she hadn't lost the suit. Earlier she'd become disgusted that she was actually primping, and had twisted her hair into a ballerina bun on top of her head. A pin was currently poking her scalp.

''This is delicious chicken, Mrs. Boswell,'' Jack said between bites. ''What's your secret?''

''It's no secret. Just a touch of rosemary and marjoram, is all.''

"It's very good," he said. "Don't you think so, Ellin?"

"What?" Darn it! He'd caught her staring at the little polo player embroidered on his crisply starched oxford shirt. "Oh, the chicken. Yes, it's definitely tasty." She forked a bite into her mouth for emphasis.

"How's the play coming along, Jack?" Ida Faye asked.

"The same as every year. Two weeks before we open I'm convinced the whole production will go down in history as the biggest fiasco ever. Then a week before, I start to think they might actually pull it off. By opening night, they've got it all together and do just fine. I hope you're planning to attend this year's performance."

"Wouldn't miss it for the world." Ida Faye explained that for the past few years Jack had directed all the student productions. "What play are you putting on?"

"It's called *Raymond and Julianne.* It's a spoof of *Romeo and Juliet,* set in a nineteenth-century Ozark village."

"I've never heard of it," Ellin said. "Who wrote it?"

"My accelerated English class," he said.

"With a lot of help from you, I'd wager." Ida Faye reached across the table and patted his arm. "Jack wrote the funniest play last year. People talked about it for ages."

Ellin watched him "aw-shucks" her grandmother's compliment. He was a playwright? As well as a teacher, novelist, reporter, volunteer fire fighter and washing machine repairman? What did the man do for a hobby? Brain surgery?

Ellin and her grandmother washed the dishes while Jack read Lizzie a story. Once she was tucked into bed, Ida Faye announced she was going to turn in, too.

"But it's only eight o'clock." Ellin didn't want to be left alone with Jack while he repaired the washing machine.

"I reckon I plumb wore myself out with all that cooking.'' Ida Faye told them to have a good night and hobbled off to her room.

Ellin reluctantly followed Jack out to the utility room where he set down the toolbox he'd brought with him. He asked her questions about the washer's malfunction as he unbuttoned his shirt and laid it aside. The snow white T-shirt he wore beneath it revealed incredibly buffed-up arms and shoulders. Who would have thought writing on chalkboards would result in such well-defined muscles? She sighed as he heaved the machine away from the wall, checked the connections, ran some water into the tub and fiddled with the hoses.

He opened the toolbox and removed a big wrench and an industrial-strength flashlight. He asked her to hold the light while he tightened...something. She wasn't actually paying attention to the sequence of repair events. He'd lost her about the time he took off his polo player. God, there was something sexy about a man in an undershirt wielding a big tool like he knew exactly how to use it.

''What?'' He must have asked her a question, but she had no idea what it was. Thinking about tools had sent her imagination down some interesting paths. In overdrive.

''Hand me that roll of duct tape, will you?'' he repeated.

His fingers brushed hers as he took it from her and she felt like she'd been zapped by a jolt of low-voltage electricity. She backed away from the danger and folded her arms across her chest. Uh-oh. She was having those crazy, lusty urges again. She should excuse herself and run straight to her room where she could barricade herself behind closed doors and heavy furniture. If she didn't, something naughty was going to happen.

She didn't move. Heck, she could barely breathe.

Jack stood up and put his tools away. ''That should take care of the problem, but I think I'd better run a load to make sure. Do you mind?'' He looked askance at the basket of clothes in the corner.

All that and he did laundry, too? Was there no end to the man's talents? ''Be my guest.''

He opened the washer and began emptying the contents of the basket into the tub. Too late, Ellin realized it included several pairs of her underwear. She made a dive for them, but she was too late. He poured in a cup of detergent and closed the lid. When he turned to her, he had smirky little grin on his face.

''You know, in all my fantasies about you, and I'll admit they have been numerous, I always imagined you in the silky stuff from Victoria's Secret. Now I see I'm going to have to revise my dreams in favor of the three-pack cotton specials from Sears.''

She wanted to be mad at him, but she didn't have the power. All she could think about was how damned hot he looked in that T-shirt washing her underwear. Maybe it was time to give in to those foolish impulses.

Yes. It was.

She didn't stop to consider the consequences of her actions. She yanked his undershirt out of his jeans with both hands and indulged in a little fantasy of her own. Slipping her hands under the thin cotton fabric, she palmed the smooth, hard muscles of his chest.

He groaned and pulled her to him. Before she could think a rational thought, his mouth found hers, and he laid another hot one on her. But this time she was ready. She laid one back. Her lips parted, and his tongue darted into her mouth. His sensual exploration took her breath away, and she gasped with pleasure at the intimacy of his touch.

Jack deepened the kiss and felt Ellin strain against him. Necking in Ida Faye's utility room was not something he had planned, but hey, there was nothing wrong with spontaneity. She ran her hands up to his shoulders, pushing him back on the washing machine. Without losing lip contact, he lifted her and sat her down on top of it. Then he reached behind her, set the controls for a short cycle and punched it on.

Their kisses were so hot and hungry they didn't break for air while the water swooshed into the tub. But then the agitator began to churn and the top of the machine shuddered in a most provocative way. Ellin moaned. Jack groaned. He didn't think he would make it all the way to spin.

With his lips melded to hers, he caressed her back through the soft shirt, then reached up and worked the pins out of her hair. They pinged onto the washer for Ida Faye to find, and the tightly coiled mass tumbled down like a silken waterfall. He buried his hands in it and cupped the delicate bones of her skull.

Ellin reciprocated by raking her fingers through Jack's tousled hair. How long had she wanted to do that? Only since the first time she'd seen him without his Santa wig. He smelled so darned nice, and his body was so big and warm. Her blood turned to liquid fire as it coursed through her veins, placing her in imminent danger of spontaneous combustion.

And she was sitting on a machine that was churning its way through the wash cycle. The steady motion vibrated a spot that had been unattended for so long she'd almost forgotten it was there. Now it was all excited and throbbing for fulfillment. Damn. Ellin had never considered herself an easy woman, but there was no doubt in her mind at the moment. She could be had.

And on top of the washing machine, no less.

Jack felt the same sense of urgency as Ellin. He didn't know exactly how they'd gotten from point A to point C without ever connecting to point B, but there was some powerful chemistry at work here. However, this was not the time, and the laundry room was certainly not the place.

Feeling like the biggest martyr in the history of martyrdom, he pulled his lips away from hers and buried his face against her neck. The washing machine made its final spin and settled into still silence.

"Wow," he said after a few seconds. His body hadn't quite gotten the message that the fun was over.

"I can't believe we just did that." Her laugh was a self-conscious attempt at normalcy.

"It kind of took me by surprise, too. I may give up teaching and go into washer repair full-time."

He sounded so serious, she had to laugh again. Then she straightened her shirt, closed a loosened button and rearranged her ruffles. She mustn't forget that in a few short weeks, she'd be gone. "I hope you don't think that what just happened actually changes anything."

"Oh, but it does," he said with a heavy sigh as he tucked his shirt into his pants. "I'll never be able to look at laundry quite the same way again."

# Chapter Eight

"Lucy, you got some 'splainin' to do." Jack used his best Ricky Ricardo accent and tossed a rumpled copy of the morning's *Post-Ette* onto Ellin's desk. If he had to grade her deportment since their little kiss-fest last week, he'd have to give her an A+ in aloofness and a "needs improvement" in approachability.

Being a sensitive soul, he'd maintained a low profile for days, trying to stay out of her space until she got her knickers unknotted. She was genetically predisposed to assume command, so the intensity of her feelings that night in the utility room had probably frightened her. The loss of control that had compelled her to dive under his shirt must have stricken raw terror into her heart.

But enough was enough.

She was a study of indifference as she dragged her gaze from the computer keyboard long enough to glance at the folded paper. "Well, that would be an editorial. Editors write them."

"I realize that. But it's a bit irresponsible, don't you

think?'' He'd sputtered in his coffee when he read her op-ed piece in the faculty lounge this morning. He still couldn't believe she would come out in favor of a gaming corporation's proposal to build a bingo hall in town. His surprise had simmered all day, and finally boiled down to perplexed aggravation.

He didn't know why she'd taken such a stand. She had heard him speak ardently against the issue at the last city council meeting. No matter how he looked at it, her printed endorsement seemed more like a personal jab at Jack Madden than a political position.

"No, actually I don't think it's irresponsible at all," she said. "I did my research. This particular company has a good record of funneling money back into the community and hiring locally to fill jobs. Like any other new business, a bingo parlor will broaden the tax base and increase city revenues. Look around you, this town could use an economic shot in the arm."

"I saw you taking notes at the meeting." He pushed his glasses into a more comfortable position. "Can I assume you were actually listening when I spoke to the council?" He'd done his homework as well, presenting convincing research that in other small communities with new gaming operations, the influx of outside elements had boosted the incidence of crime, including shoplifting, theft and assault. Many in town shared his views and didn't think increasing revenues was worth the cost.

She swiveled her chair around to face him. "I heard what you had to say, Madden. It just so happens that I disagree with you. I am allowed to do that, aren't I?"

"Throwing your editorial weight around, is more like it."

She turned back to her computer. "God bless America," she said with a mocking salute. "Where everyone is enti-

tled to an opinion, no matter how uninformed and misguided it may be.''

"Why are you doing this?" he demanded. "You keep
saying you're only going to be here until the end of
March.''

"That's right." She made a show of consulting her desk
calendar. "Lucky me. Less than sixty days to go. And
counting.''

Her comment was a pointed reminder that time was running out. And they were still at cross-purposes. The thought
affected him like a gut-punch. "So why champion something that's obviously wrong for a town you plan to leave
anyway?''

"Maybe it's not obvious to me.''

He had other arguments prepared but knew it would be
fruitless, not to mention counterproductive, to toss them
into the ring. "Maybe this isn't about bingo at all.''

"Oh? So what's it about then?''

He noticed Deanie Sue trying hard to look disinterested
in the heated exchange taking place only four feet from her
desk.

"I think it's about…laundry," he said triumphantly. And
the flaming passions that had erupted atop Mt. Maytag.

Ellin scoffed. "*You* wish!''

"That's it, isn't it?" He couldn't keep the smugness out
of his voice. "This is no more than a diversionary tactic.
You're just throwing up defenses. Battening down the old
Bennett hatches. You think if you can make me mad
enough, it'll distract me from the real issue.''

"You're arrogant *and* insane," she said with a dismis-
sive snort. "Believe it or not, everything is not about you.''

"Maybe not," he allowed. "But this is. Isn't it?''

"No, Madden." She shoved the keyboard tray under the
desktop in a full-blown snit. "I'll tell you what it is about,

though. This is about my belief system being in direct and fatal conflict with yours."

"Right."

"Period."

"Okay." He shrugged. "If telling yourself that helps you sleep."

She picked up a pencil and pointed it at him like a miniature javelin before tossing it down with a frustrated sigh. "It also points up some fundamental and important differences between us."

He leaned on her desk, his hands planted palms down, mere inches from her face. "And what, pray tell, would those differences be?"

He had to give her credit. Ellin Bennett wasn't a give up or give out woman. She got right back in his face. Fortunately, he found her spirit highly arousing.

"For starters," she said, "I can see the big picture and you can't. I think outside the box and you don't. I acknowledge that a world exists beyond Washington, Arkansas, and you aren't willing to."

If he weren't so frustrated, and if Deanie Sue weren't watching with quite so much curiosity, he would kiss Ellin right now, just to shut her up and fan the flames. Instead, he threw down the gauntlet.

"Prove it."

"What did you say?" she asked in quiet fury.

"You heard me. Put up or shut up. I am all for doing another load of laundry. Anytime. Any place. Are you?"

He saw Ellin glance at Deanie Sue who seemed confused by the ferocity with which they were discussing such a mundane topic. She put her hands on her desk and leaned forward, nearly coming up out of her chair. Lowering her voice only put more sting into her words.

"I wouldn't do laundry with you, Jack Madden, if you were the last man on the planet."

"I don't believe you."

"I don't care."

"Oh, you care all right," he said. "See, you *need* to do laundry. In fact, your biggest problem is that you've been letting your laundry pile up for a long time now. I think you are seriously overdue for a good sudsing."

Her eyes widened in shock, then narrowed in outraged indignation. "Is that right?"

"Yep."

"Well, let me tell you the nice thing about laundry, Madden. I can take care of it myself. I don't need you, or any other man, to assist me in my sudsing activities."

He grinned, licked his finger and made an imaginary mark on an imaginary score board. She was good. A fellow with a more fragile ego would be running for the nearest corner to count his *cajones*. Jack headed for the door, content to let her win this round. But he would leave her with something to ponder.

"Fine by me, Bennett. Just don't go rummaging around in my toolbox the next time your washing machine needs tweaking."

Jack's parting shot launched Ellin into a tailspin that lasted all afternoon as she made the rounds selling ads and collecting tidbits of news. As if that weren't enough, everywhere she went, someone made a crack about the speeding ticket that was now a matter of public record. The notice had appeared in the "Legal News" column of the *Post-Ette,* ostensibly to warn innocent motorists to be on the alert for dangerous and irresponsible maniacs.

Like her twenty-eight miles per hour posed a serious threat to public safety or warranted her being called "Leadfoot" by the general populace. And she could do without all the slyly pointed "vroom-vroom" sound effects.

En route to Hess's Hardware to see the owner about his anniversary sale ad, she walked past the Value-Dollar Store. She glanced in the window and the colorful display of red plastic detergent bottles prompted an unwanted and unnerving memory. Was there no escaping the man or the reminders of her own foolish impulses?

What was it about Jack Madden anyway? How did he get to be so...perfect? Others might call him a jack-of-all-trades. A regular Ozark renaissance man. But to her he was the grain of sand in her oyster of life. He was constantly irritating her, but somehow he always managed to turn that irritation into some kind of gem. She'd never met anyone like him. Heck, there *weren't* any other men like him. He was definitely one of a kind. Which, she had to admit, was part of the problem. He was also right. She *had* been letting her laundry pile up. For a couple of years now.

Mr. Hess was just closing up after his departing employees when she got there. He invited her in and outlined how he wanted the twenty-fifth anniversary sale spread to look. She sketched it out for him and asked questions for a short general interest piece to accompany the ad.

"Are you all right, Mr. Hess?" she asked when she noticed a flicker of pain on his pale face.

He pressed a clenched fist to his chest. "It's this dadgum indigestion. I had sauerkraut and sausage at the diner for lunch. Gets me every time."

Ellin took notes, but watched him closely as he told her how he'd started the company on a shoestring with money he'd made plucking chickens at the processing plant. He told her he didn't believe in retirement. He planned to keep working until they carried him out feet first.

Which, she worried, might happen at any minute. She

didn't like the clammy way he looked. She'd never heard of heartburn so severe it caused the sufferer to break out in a cold sweat.

"I'm sorry, Ms. Bennett. I believe I need to sit myself down." Alvie Hess turned away to pull out a desk chair, clapped his hand to his chest and promptly collapsed on the floor.

She dropped to her knees beside him. "Mr. Hess!" The sixty-year-old's eyes fluttered, and he gasped for breath, unable to speak. "Hang on, sir, I'll call 911."

She pulled the phone off the desk and punched in the emergency number. She turned back to the fallen man as soon as she'd given the dispatcher the problem and location. Speaking quietly to reassure him, she folded her coat and placed it under his head. She didn't know what else to do. She'd always intended to take CPR training, in fact it had been offered several times by her former employer's staff development people. She just had not taken the time out of her overtaxed schedule to complete the course.

She began to panic. Mr. Hess's breathing was becoming increasingly labored, his face gray and damp. How long would it take an ambulance to get here?

Jack had stayed late at school to grade essays and was on his way home when he received the call. As one of the four first responders in town, he notified the dispatcher by radio that he was less than two minutes from the fire station and would make the run. When he arrived, he quickly unlocked the metal building housing the volunteer fire department's headquarters, jumped in the emergency equipment truck and headed for Hess's Hardware.

Luckily, many of the businesses on Main street had already closed for the day, so he was able to park right in front of the store. He grabbed the first aid bag and the automated external defibrillator and ran inside.

He hadn't anticipated finding Ellin kneeling beside Alvie Hess. She looked up and the surprise on her face matched his own.

"Jack? What are you doing here?"

"Not now." He was obviously the last person she had expected to show up and save a life, but he didn't have time to explain. Alvie didn't look good. His skin was ashen, his lips tinged with blue. Jack went to work immediately, assessing his condition and choosing the best course of action. He snapped on a pair of latex gloves and pressed his fingers against Alvie's carotid artery. He palpated a thready pulse, but before he could complete a count, it ceased abruptly, plunging the owner of the hardware store into sudden cardiac arrest.

Jack switched on the automated external defibrillator which was easy to operate, and ripped Alvie's shirt open. The machine could determine on its own whether the patient required a shock to halt the heart's lethal arrhythmia, or ventricular fibrillation. Alvie Hess's heart was clearly in v-fib. Jack triggered the machine when prompted, making sure Ellin wasn't touching the patient when the shock was delivered.

After the third assault, Alvie's heart resumed its normal contraction rhythms. Once a pattern was established, Jack placed an oxygen mask over the patient's nose and mouth to assist his breathing. Then he sat back on his heels and grinned up at Ellin.

"He's going to make it."

It was another fifteen minutes before the ambulance from Fayetteville arrived. Ellin watched as the paramedics loaded the patient for the trip to the hospital. He was alert and although his mouth was covered by the oxygen mask, he tried to thank Jack who squeezed his hand and told him he was going to be just fine. He promised to call Alvie's wife Edith so she could meet him at the hospital.

Ellin had covered many rescue stories in her career, but she had always maintained the necessary professional detachment. Never had she been so close to the drama, or so deeply moved by its outcome. Jack Madden had saved another human's life as easily as most men might fill their gas tanks. He made it seem like an everyday occurrence, but it more than that. It was a miracle.

He had made a stopped heart beat again, had restored a husband to his wife, given a father back to his children. He'd acted selflessly to help a friend. But she knew with certainty that Jack would have done the same for a total stranger.

"Do you think he'll really be all right?" she asked over the retreating siren.

"I'm no doctor, but I think he has a better than even chance. Studies show that people who survive a sudden cardiac arrest have a good long-term outlook."

"I hope so. He's a really nice man."

"Statistically, something like eighty-three percent are alive at one year. Nearly fifty-seven percent make it to five years."

"That's incredible."

"Not really," he said. "It's medical science. There's been a push in recent years to get the AEDs into local rescue services and to educate people through community programs. Washington is small, but we have four first responders with forty hours of emergency medical training each. We get to the scene of an accident first and keep the victims alive until the EMS guys get there."

"And it's all voluntary?"

He nodded and borrowed a cell phone from a bystander

to call Mr. Hess's wife. He explained what had happened and assured her in his quiet, confidence-inspiring voice that Alvie was going to be all right.

"Why do you do it?" She'd never met anyone who did as much for others. And he did it for purely unselfish reasons.

"To help people, I guess. A small town is like a big family. You know everyone, and you do what you can. That could have been my dad in that ambulance. Or Ida Faye."

She smiled. "Were you the first to respond when she broke her hip?"

"I was closest."

That explained a few things. No wonder there was such a strong bond between her grandmother and the gallant young man. He was the knight in shining armor who had come to her rescue when she slipped on the ice and cried for help.

The small crowd gathered on the street slowly dispersed. Several people clapped Jack on the back and commended him for his quick actions. He downplayed his role, saying he was just glad he'd been in the right place at the right time.

Ellin accompanied him as he replaced his equipment in the emergency truck.

"That's an amazing machine," she said of the automated external defibrillator.

"We just got it a few months ago. This is the first time I've had to use it."

"You looked like an old hand at it to me."

"It's idiot-proof. That's what makes it so useful to non-medical people like volunteer fire departments. With it, we can save more lives, because the sooner a heart is restarted, the better the chances of recovery. The truth is, chances for survival are reduced by nearly ten percent with every minute of delay."

She followed him inside to turn off the lights and lock the store. She was still trying to squeeze him into one of the tight little character compartments she'd devised over the years. He simply would not fit. He picked up her coat from the floor and held it so she could slip into it.

"Put this on," Jack told her. "You're shivering." He pulled the heavy wool coat around her shoulders and tugged it closed. He stopped just short of buttoning the buttons when he saw the soft light shining in her eyes. When they misted over, he knew she was not trembling from the cold but from an avalanche of unfamiliar emotions.

He opened his arms and she stepped into them, burying her face against his chest. He embraced her as she wept quietly, stroking her hair and whispering reassurances. God, how he'd longed for this moment. When duke-it-out-at-all-costs Ellin Bennett would come to him willingly, seeking the solace and protection he so wanted to give her. He tightened his hold on her. How would he survive if she made good on her promise to leave? He couldn't bear it if she rejected his world and returned to her own.

He held her face in his hands and turned it up to his. "Are you all right?"

She nodded. "I'm sorry. I guess I was overwhelmed by, well, everything."

"Rescue work can be overwhelming. It's not for sissies," he said with a smile.

She started to laugh, but it caught on a sob. "*You* overwhelm me, Jack. You do so much. Give so much to others. And you don't expect anything in return. You do it because you can, and because it's right. You're Santa Claus all year round."

He caressed her hair and smoothed a loose strand behind her ear. "People need people, Ellin. So do you."

No. She had always considered needing to be a sure shortcut to unhappiness. She'd taught herself long ago to be self-reliant, and not to depend on anyone for anything. She was a newcomer at the giving table, but Jack Madden made her want to practice until she got it right.

"You're too good to be true, you know," she whispered.

He cupped her face between his hands and lowered his lips slowly to hers. He kissed her softly, longingly, as though savoring each nuance of taste and sensation. She kissed him back just as tenderly, exulting in the intense desire that shocked her heart as surely as the defibrillator had shocked Alvie Hess's. Only instead of being restored to normal, her heart raced in excited discovery.

What she felt with Jack was very special. Even she was smart enough to realize that. It was an ache so exquisite that it produced pain and pleasure at the same time. It was something so wonderful she had never believed it existed. She wished it had never started. Yet she didn't want it to ever end. She was terrified by what it promised.

Ellin was clumsy and inexperienced in matters of love, but as Jack deepened the kiss, and put his own heart into it, she knew exactly what he was offering. She was honored that he thought her worthy of such an incredible gift, but she was also afraid to accept it. She could never be responsible for something so rare and valuable.

Whatever the cost, she knew it was better to refuse his heart now, than to break it later.

## Chapter Nine

Ellin decided to sell small heart-shaped personal ads in the Valentine's Day issue of the *Post-Ette*. It started out as a marketing ploy to sell a few extra newspapers, but soon grew into a local phenomenon. Being more pragmatic than romantic, she never suspected so many sentimental, love-sick souls would line up to display their innermost feelings in a public forum. Or be so willing to pay for the privilege.

To lend an aura of mystery to the Be Mine campaign, Deanie Sue decorated a box with colorful hearts and placed it on the counter in the office. The lovelorn simply filled out a form and dropped it, along with the five-dollar fee, into the box. Those with deeper feelings and bigger budgets bought full-size ads at the regular rate, which significantly increased profits for the month.

Traffic at The Love Box, as it soon became known around town, was steady during the two weeks prior to the holiday. The first customers were mostly high school and junior high students, but as word got out, a more diverse group began to stop by. Apparently, no one wanted their significant other to feel left out or unloved on Cupid's big day. By the time the issue went to print, Ellin had expanded the Be Mine section to two full pages.

She authorized the printing of two hundred additional copies of the Valentine's Day edition, which was her sixth since taking over as editor. By Wednesday afternoon, the extras were sold out. Everyone in town wanted to read the printed declarations of love, and decoding messages inscribed with initials became a favorite pastime.

Deanie Sue couldn't stop grinning as she prepared the bank deposit that afternoon. Not only had the ads turned out to be a sweetheart deal for the paper, but to her never-ending surprise someone had placed one that read "To D.S.M. You are worshipped from afar. I hope someday you will be mine."

Because of the anonymity factor, she had no idea who might be infatuated with her. But that only seemed to increase her pleasure. The widow said having a secret admirer, who might choose to reveal himself at any time, gave her something to look forward to each day. Maybe she would start wearing makeup again.

Ellin had been too busy to review the ads that came in just before deadline. She gave Owen carte blanche approval on the final layout of the special section and he took the added responsibility seriously. He used all the flowery fonts and frilly hearts clip art he could find.

"So who do you think has the hots for you, Deanie Sue?" Ellin had a pretty good idea of the mystery man's identity. She'd seen Owen gazing longingly at the bookkeeper when he thought no one was looking.

The older woman blushed. "Mercy me, I'd hardly call it that." Then she giggled, something she was not generally prone to do. "But just knowing someone out there is thinking about you *is* kind of exciting, isn't it?"

"I wouldn't know about that." Ellin began clearing off her desk. She'd never really liked Valentine's Day. It wasn't a real holiday anyway, just something retailers trumped up to promote consumer spending. She especially didn't like the fact that she, as unsentimental and practical as a woman could be, had actually been born on February 14th.

The older woman pored over the Be Mine ads. "What's your middle name, El?"

"Elizabeth, why?"

"Because there's an ad in here that might be intended for you."

"I doubt that." She looked where Deanie Sue pointed. "To E.E.B., It Will All Come Out In The Wash. Don Quixote" was scrawled in lacy script across a double-sized ad. She thought of the incident with Jack in the laundry room and was infused with a slow heat. She'd never told him her middle name, but he had to be responsible for this. An English teacher would know an obscure quote from a famous piece of literature.

"It says it's from Don Kwixote," Deanie Sue mispronounced. "I don't believe he's from around here. Do you know anyone by that name?"

"No," she said with a smile. "Not personally."

"Of course, it could be for Emily Eileen Brown," Deanie Sue speculated. "She's glee club captain at the high school this year. This Don guy might be one of those basketball players from over at Hilldale."

"Yes, that's probably it."

The older woman continued to scan the paper. "Oh, my. Here's another one. 'To E.E.B., There Is a Tide In the Affairs of Men. Julius Caesar.' Now, I know that's no local boy."

Ellin groaned when she realized the significance of the

quotes. Jack was definitely up to no good. The meaning of the washing reference was clear. And tide? He knew what brand of laundry detergent she used.

"El, there's one more. But I really don't get this one." She read the message. "'To E.E.B., That's where I reckon Santa Claus comes in. Robert Frost.' Isn't he somebody famous?"

"He's an American poet," Ellin explained. "That line is from, um, 'Plane to Plane' I believe."

"Oh. That doesn't seem like something a basketball player would know anything about." Deanie Sue removed her purse from her drawer as she prepared to leave for the day.

"No, it doesn't." She smiled. But it sounded exactly like something Jack would know about.

Owen stepped out of the back room and offered to walk the bookkeeper to her car. Ellin watched as he held her coat and then the door in a most courtly manner. She was convinced Owen Larsen had penned the secret Be Mine message that had set the older woman all atwitter. The two had been co-workers for over ten years, but as far as she knew he had never before stepped out from behind his mask of shyness.

Feeling a Cupid-like satisfaction, Ellin picked up the paper and reread the messages addressed to E.E.B. There was no doubt in her mind who had placed those ads. Maybe she hadn't mentioned her middle name, but any man as accomplished as Jack would have no trouble with a bit of simple detective work.

He'd asked her out often since her emotions had gotten the best of her in Hess's Hardware, but she'd turned down any invitation remotely resembling a date. When they spent time together, Lizzie was always there to chaperone.

Her precocious daughter had sat between them at a Sat-

urday matinee of the latest kiddie film. She had suckered
them into endless rounds of Chutes and Ladders on Ida
Faye's living room floor. She'd instigated a trip to Mama
Maria's for pizza and video games. She'd held their hands
during a tour of the Maddens' hen houses and had shared
Sunday dinner at their table.

Ellin enjoyed the outings as much as Lizzie. Jack was
fun to be with, articulate and quick with a quip. He was
well-read, and curious about a wide variety of subjects.
She'd even learned to accept his laid-back style because
she knew he would not be the same man if he changed. He
was still the grain of sand in her oyster, both frustrating
and exasperating at times. But he was the most stimulating
person she'd ever known, and he never failed to make her
laugh.

Every time she was with him, she learned to appreciate
life a little more. Ellin still didn't understand why he was
content to remain in peaceful little Washington, when a big,
fascinating world beckoned beyond its boundaries. But
she'd come to accept the fact that he was.

Like Lizzie, Ellin looked forward to Jack's company, but
she was careful never to be alone with him. She'd convinced herself that by avoiding intimate contact and personal issues, she could keep their relationship on a nonsex-
ual and therefore, nonthreatening basis.

It was a tough balancing act. She had to work without a
net as he figured prominently in her daydreams and fantasies. But sex and/or mushy stuff would only complicate
things. So she was constantly wrestling her feelings of desire into a more tolerable form of affection.

Jack was important to her and Lizzie, and Ellin didn't
want to hurt him any more than she wanted to *be* hurt.
She'd realized what was at stake that day he'd kissed her
so tenderly after saving Alvie Hess's life. Ellin didn't want

to give up the only real friend she'd ever had. And Lizzie shouldn't have to give up her hero when they moved on. After ten years in journalism, she'd seen much that was wrong with the world. Dealing daily with the headlined results of society's apathy and cruelty had hardened her cynical heart.

But Jack Madden had come along and restored her faith in her fellow man. He was one of the truly good guys. A light in a dark world. Knowing that men like him existed made her optimistic about the future of the planet.

She could keep the relationship alive via phone calls, e-mails, letters and occasional visits, so long as it remained platonic and unsullied by serious emotions. She knew from unfortunate experience that long-distance love affairs were doomed from the start. Her failed marriage was all the proof she needed.

Ellin felt less vulnerable once she made up her mind not to become physically involved with Jack. Drawing an invisible line between them gave her a sense of peace, and she wasn't as troubled by frightening, out-of-control feelings. For the past few weeks, she'd been successful at keeping their shared activities on the safe side of the divide.

When he tried to get close, she stepped back. When he tried to reel her in by being his ever-adorable self, she concentrated on her long-term goals in order to etch the division more firmly in her mind. She had to be strong. Half her allotted time in Washington was over. Work was an important part of her life, and when Jig Baker resumed leadership of the *Post-Ette,* there would be nothing for her to do here.

She'd sent out a sheaf of résumés to newspapers all over the country. Some had replied expressing interest in what she had to offer. Despite the brief detour in Arkansas, her future was on track again. She had her eyes back on the prize.

Jack Madden was an utterly charming distraction, and she would never knowingly hurt him. But she was the mature one here. It was up to her to set limits and make sure good sense was not overwhelmed by desire. There was only one way to do that.

She could never, ever, cross the line.

Jack caught up with her just as she was getting into her car to go home. "Editor Ellin! Where are you off to?"

She turned to him with a smile. So that's what the E. E. in the ads stood for. "Yes, Don Quixote Caesar Frost?"

He snapped his fingers in a darn-it-all gesture. "You mean you figured it out already?"

"Hey, you're dealing with an award-winning investigative reporter here, you know."

"Oh, yeah. I keep forgetting. So where are you headed?"

"Home."

"How would you like to go to a barn burning? It'll be really fun, and you can get a story out of it for next week's paper."

"I've heard of barnyards and barn dances, barn swallows and barn raisings. But I don't believe I'm familiar with the term barn burning. What exactly does that involve?"

"Well, it's fairly self-explanatory. Bill Cranston was planning to tear down his old barn to make way for a new one." Jack grinned and rubbed his hands in exaggerated glee. "But I talked him into letting the volunteer fire department burn it down instead."

"I see. Some kind of rustic Valentine's Day ritual?"

"Nope. We just need to practice putting out a big fire. We were going to do it yesterday, but it was too windy.

Want to go? I look really macho in my bunker suit wielding
that big hose.''

It was an intriguing proposition that conjured up images
she preferred not to think about. ''Sure, why not? Let me
get my camera so I can record the event for future gener-
ations.''

They left Ellin's car parked where it was and Jack drove
to the Cranston farm which was located a few miles north
of town. Most of the twenty-two-man volunteer fire-
fighting brigade had already assembled around the tumble-
down barn. The livestock had been removed to a back pas-
ture where they would not be frightened by the flames.

Jack quickly donned his protective yellow suit, boots,
gloves and helmet. He gave Ellin a big grin before snapping
down his face shield and went to work helping his brother-
in-law Ted McGovern unreel the fire hose from the truck.
Two water tankers stood at the ready.

It was a cold day and Ellin turned up her collar as she
walked around snapping photos. Fire Chief Hal Madden
directed the volunteers to incinerate and then extinguish a
roaring blaze that completely destroyed the structure. The
old barn was a ramshackle tinderbox so the entire process,
from beginning to end, took less than an hour. It was dusk
by the time they'd pumped a sufficient amount of water on
the pile of smoldering ashes to prevent sparks from reig-
niting. The men commended each other for a job well done
and began putting away their equipment.

Ellin was repacking her camera when Jack called out to
her. She turned and watched appreciatively as he sauntered
through the twilight toward her, his long-limbed body
bulked up in the protective gear. He carried his helmet under his arm, but had not yet removed the fire-retardant hood
he wore under it. The sight of his soot-smeared face and
big, goofy grin made her heart surge. Despite her vow to

keep their relationship platonic, she couldn't help wanting him.

She clapped in recognition of his efforts, then reached out, removed his glasses and wiped them on a tissue from her coat pocket.

He bowed from the waist. "Were you suitably impressed?"

"I'll say. You were all over the place." She replaced his glasses and clamped a dramatic hand over her racing heart. "That had to be the most thrilling display of he-man machismo I have witnessed in recent years."

"Ugh. That good." He pounded his chest in a Tarzan-like display of male dominance, but ruined the Neanderthal effect with a tutorial. "According to well-accepted anthropological theories, females are genetically driven to choose males they perceive capable of defending them against danger and predators. It's nature's way of encouraging reproduction and insuring propagation of the species."

"Is that so?"

"Yep." He winked in a broadly lascivious manner. Then he leaned down and whispered, "Give me a minute to get out of this outfit, and I promise I'll stand still while you exercise your procreative imperative all over me."

She smiled sweetly. "Thanks for the offer, but I think I'll go talk to the men. I need some information for my story."

Jack shrugged. "All right. If you don't want to do your part to aid the survival of mankind..." He sighed as Ellin walked away, her hips swinging in a most provocative way. Maybe she didn't know what she did to him, but it was difficult to keep up the banter when all he wanted to do was pull her down on the ground and make wild monkey love with her.

The last few weeks had set him back considerably. Double-dating with Lizzie didn't give him many opportunities to tell Ellin how he felt. He smiled. Maybe he wouldn't tell her. A picture was supposed to be worth a thousand words. *Showing* her would be far more fun.

And when better to do that than on Valentine's Day? All he needed was a little luck and the aid of the patron saint of lovers. Time was ticking down. He only had six more weeks, so tonight he would have to kick ''The Plan'' into high gear.

Ellin was tucking her notebook into her camera bag as she rejoined him. ''I think this'll make an interesting story.''

''Did you get everything you needed?'' He stowed his gear in his truck and opened the door for her.

''Yes. Your father was very helpful.'' She climbed in and when he started the engine, she glanced at the dashboard clock. ''Oh, no! I'm late picking up Lizzie. Mrs. Kendall will be wondering what happened to me.''

He turned onto the road and headed for town. ''Actually, I took the liberty of asking Jana to drop Lizzie off at Ida Faye's.

''You did?''

''I wasn't sure how long we'd be at the fire. I hope you don't mind.''

''Well, no. I appreciate the thought. I'll still make it home in time to fix dinner.''

''I sort of delivered them a pizza earlier. Double cheese. Lizzie's favorite. They've probably eaten it by now.''

He took them a pizza? ''All right,'' she said suspiciously. ''What's going on here?''

''It's Valentine's Day.''

''Yeah, so?''

''So, since we're the closest thing either of us have to a

sweet patootie, I think we should spend the evening together.''

"A sweet what?" she asked in consternation.

"Patootie. It's a slang term for sweetheart. Surely you've
heard it used before."

"Not by anyone who wasn't a cartoon character."

"Well, be that as it may, I am cooking you dinner and
to make it worth your while, maybe I'll show you my sax."

"Your what?"

"Saxophone. Didn't I mention that I played in the University of Arkansas marching band?"

"It must have slipped your mind. Thanks for the offer,"
she said, "but I should probably go home."

"Do you realize you've never been inside my house?"

"There's a good reason for that," she muttered.

"Are you afraid of being alone with me, Ellin?" He
looked over at her, a challenge in his eyes and in his tone.
"That's it, isn't it?"

"No. Of course not."

"Are you worried I might take advantage of you?"

"No-o-o."

"Ah, you're worried you might take advantage of me."

"I just don't think it's a good idea, that's all."

He drove past her parked car and turned down a quiet
tree-lined avenue. "Too bad. It's gone way beyond the idea
stage. It's pretty much a done deal at this point."

She didn't put up much of a fight. She knew from past
experience that it was no fun to be alone on her birthday.
In less than an hour, Lizzie and Ida Faye would be in bed
and she'd be sitting there cursing herself for not taking Jack
up on his offer. But the problem was, she didn't know what
he was offering.

"I'll make you a deal," he said as he pulled into the
driveway of a modified Georgian-style house. "I hereby

promise to control my wildest impulses, if you will promise to control yours.''

Ellin looked around Jack's living room while he was upstairs showering off the fire-fighting grime. How many times had she told herself not to be surprised by anything the man did? And yet she hadn't expected a bachelor's home to be so comfortable. The eighty-year-old redbrick house had a white-columned portico, lead-paned windows and an old-fashioned fanlight over the front door. It was the kind of house a doctor or a banker might have built back in the twenties.

Twelve-foot ceilings and smooth red oak floors gave the large rooms an old-fashioned charm. Oriental rugs and an eclectic mix of modern and antique furnishings and paintings made them warm and inviting. She smiled when she saw the tenor saxophone on a stand in the corner. Sheet music lay scattered on a mahogany music rest nearby. He owed her a demonstration of his musical abilities.

Ellin stood before the crackling fire Jack had built when they came in and studied the framed photographs on the mantel. She recognized a much younger Hal and Mary in their wedding clothes and Jack and Jana at various stages of development. Big-eyed toddlers in a Radio Flyer wagon. Sturdy ten-year-olds on a tire swing. Grinning graduates in mortarboards at their high school ceremony. It seemed they'd always been close.

''Can I get you a drink?''

She whirled around at the sound of his voice, but it wasn't the sudden movement that made her breath catch in her throat. He was dressed in faded jeans and a pale blue V-necked sweater that looked soft enough to be cashmere. The sleeves were pushed up to his elbows, baring tanned forearms dusted with dark hair. He'd stepped into a pair of loafers without bothering with the formality of socks. His still-damp hair was mussed as though he considered toweling style enough.

"Wine if you have it." She didn't quite know how to act without her chatty, four-year-old chaperone. Being in Jack's house, alone with him, at night, made her nervous. Excited.

"Red or white?" he asked on his way to the kitchen.

"White, please."

He returned a few minutes later and set two glasses and an open bottle of Chenin blanc on the coffee table. "Come on, Editor Ellin, sit." He patted the couch cushion beside him. "Don't look so edgy, I won't bite. I'm saving the neck-nibbling for the entertainment portion of the program." He handed her a glass of wine.

She took it and perched on the edge of the overstuffed sofa. "Did you do the decorating? It's very nice."

"Thanks. I can't take all the credit. Jana helped me pick out some things." He aimed a remote control at an open cabinet and soft, bluesy music emanated from a CD player.

She sniffed the air. "Why does it smell so good in here? Unless you're some kind of culinary magician, you haven't been home long enough to prepare food."

He rested one ankle on the other knee and sipped his wine. "Slow cooker. Wonderful invention. I put the beef Stroganoff on this morning before I left for school. It'll be ready soon."

"You cook, too?" Ellin had always felt capable in the world of journalism. But Jack's many accomplishments made her realize just how limited her expertise was.

He gave her a doesn't-everybody-shrug. "I like to eat. Mom taught Jana and I how to cook and clean, and Dad taught us how to fix things and work on cars. My parents believe that if all boys knew how to keep house and all girls knew how to keep their cars running, no one would ever have to marry for any reason other than true love.''

She laughed. ''That's a romantic notion.''

''I come from a long line of romantics on my daddy's side. Grandpa and Grandma Madden met at a USO dance and eloped after a thirty-day acquaintance.''

''You're kidding?''

''Nope. It's a tradition in our family that when you know, you know. We're like swans. We mate for life. My parents only dated two and half months before they said 'I do.' And they've had nearly thirty years of wedded bliss—''

Nearly thirty years? ''How old *are* you anyway?''

''Don't worry, I'm legal. You didn't let me finish. According to Dad, thirty happy years out of thirty-five is nothing to sneeze at.''

''So you're actually...'' Mathematical calculations had always confused her.

He smiled. ''Thirty. Since we're sharing statistics, how old are you?''

She'd known he was younger than her, but hadn't realized there was a five-year difference in their ages. She hoped her advanced years would discourage him. ''I'm thirty-five.''

''Today. Talk about romantic. Being born on Valentine's Day gives you a definite edge over the rest of us.''

''How did you know it was my birthday?''

''It's not something I'm proud of.'' He hung his head in mock shame. ''But I wheedled it out of Ida Faye.''

''Knowing my grandmother,'' she said, ''wheedling probably was not necessary.''

''That's true. All I had to do was crank the Madden charm up a notch, and she spilled her guts. Told me everything I wanted to know, Ellin Elizabeth.''

She grinned. "Fair's fair. Now you have to tell me yours."

"November tenth."

"And your middle name."

"That would be Nathan, after Grandpa Madden. Jana's is Nadine, in honor of Grandma. My parents are big on tradition."

"I like your folks," she told him. "You're lucky to have such a close, loving family." She knew how unconnected her own life had been before coming to Washington.

"My parents have been good role models." He propped his feet on the coffee table and leaned against the cushion. "I've always wanted what they have."

"A chicken farm?" she asked with a sly grin.

"No, not a chicken farm." He swatted her lightly on the arm. "I'm trying to have a serious conversation here."

"Sorry. What is it you want, Jack?"

You, Ellin Elizabeth Bennett, he thought. I want you. Now and forever. I want to wake up every day knowing I have another twenty-four hours to love you. Those were the words Jack longed to say. But he knew it was too soon. She wasn't ready to hear them, and he could not risk jeopardizing their chance for a future together.

"I want to spend my life loving one woman," he told her. "A woman who loves only me." He leaned toward her, breathing the flowery scent of her hair. Alarm registered on her face, and she scooted down the couch, out of his reach.

"I take it you're in favor of marriage?" She grabbed one of the tasseled throw pillows Jana had spent too much of his money on and clasped it to her bosom like a long-lost child.

"I'm a major proponent of the concept." He gently removed the pillow from her grasp and made a show of restoring it to its former position.

"It works for some people, but I don't think everyone is cut out for marriage."

"Are you referring to anyone I know?"

She gave him a sad smile. "Being married wasn't the happiest time in my life. You know how much I hate to fail."

"Your ex-husband was the wrong man for you." He stretched his arm along the back of the couch. "We all have a soul mate. The person who completes us and teaches us why we were born."

She shook her head. "It's a lovely thought, but I don't believe it. What we perceive as love is just the temporary short-circuiting of brain chemicals, exacerbated by hormonal imbalance."

He made a face. "See, that's why you're not a poet."

"I'm a realist. I also learn from my mistakes."

"You just made a bad connection the first time," he told her. "He wasn't 'The One.' When you understand that it had to end, in order to free you to find your true love, it doesn't seem like a failure at all, does it?"

"That's why you *are* a poet." She wasn't comfortable debating the merits of love and marriage. Or sitting so close to the yummy-smelling man with whom she'd vowed not to get romantically involved.

"I'm good with my hands, too. And I play well with others."

She finished her wine and set the glass on the table. "When do we eat? Watching you flex your muscles out at the barn burning today really gave me an appetite."

"Very subtle change of subject there. But I'll let it go this time." He stood and pulled her to her feet. "Come on, Lois Lane, let me feed you before you collapse on me."

He started for the kitchen, then turned around and tugged her close. "On second thought, since you're a guest in my home, feel free to collapse on me at any time."

She pulled away. "You promised to mind your manners."

"That I did. And I keep my promises."

She asked him if she could use the phone to call home, and her grandmother assured her that she and Lizzie were just fine. They were playing Chutes and Ladders and would be going to bed soon. Not to worry. She should enjoy her dinner and her birthday.

Ellin suspected a conspiracy, but she didn't say so. She set the table and made a salad while Jack boiled noodles for the Stroganoff. They sipped their wine and lingered over dinner.

"There's something I've been wanting to ask you for a long time now," she said.

He set his glass down. "All right. I'll marry you."

She laughed. "That wasn't it. You mentioned once that you'd traveled in college. That you'd been to Africa. But you've never talked about it. Will you tell me now?"

The smiled faded from his face and a profoundly sad look replaced it. "There's nothing to tell, really. I went to Rwanda as a journalism intern one summer. That's it."

She sensed there was far more to the experience than he seemed willing to share but didn't want to upset him if he was uncomfortable talking about it. "Journalism? You never mentioned that was your major."

He shrugged. "I switched to education in grad school. It's a long, not very interesting, story. Remind me to tell you all about it someday."

She would. He was being evasive, but her own reporting instincts told her to ease off. She'd get more information in the long run if she didn't press for details too soon. "So tell me about the novel you're writing."

"I really don't like to talk about it. It seems to dilute my creative energy. You understand, don't you?"

"Of course. Would letting me read it dilute your creative energy?"

He grinned. "I'll think about it. Enough about me. Let's talk about Ellin."

She surprised herself by opening up to him. But he was a good listener and before she knew how they'd gotten on the subject, she was telling him about her lonely childhood and how she'd grown up without her father. That led her to bemoan her ex-husband's lack of interest in their daughter.

"He makes me so angry," she said. "He says he'll get more involved with her later, when she's older."

"How could he not want to spend time with the princess?" Jack's disbelief was genuine, he'd become quite attached to Lizzie Bennett. In fact, the thought of losing Ellin was made doubly painful when he realized that her little girl was part of the package deal. "She's such a joy."

"Andrew doesn't share your appreciation of children, not even his own."

"That's another indication that he was not the right man for you." He propped his arms on the table. "Do you still have feelings for him?"

She shook her head. "It's been over a long time. In fact, now that I've seen how happy your parents are, and how much in love Jana and Ted are, I seriously doubt that I ever really loved him at all. Not in that till-death-us-do-part way. Our marriage was a mistake."

"No, it wasn't." He touched her hand in reassurance. "It was meant to be. It gave you Lizzie."

"That's right." She stood and started stacking dishes in

the sink, running water over them. "You always make me feel better about myself. You make me understand things I never understood before. Where does your insight come from?"

"I'm an old soul. Leave those dishes." He pulled her hands out of the sink and dried them with a cotton towel. Then he led her back to the living room. "Come on. I have something far more interesting planned."

# Chapter Ten

Jack directed Ellin to sit on the couch and cautioned her to keep her eyes closed. He hurried back to the kitchen and returned with the birthday cake he'd prepared earlier. He set it on the coffee table in front of her, dimmed the lights and lit the tiny pink candles.

She had removed her shoes and sat in her stocking feet, her elbows propped on her knees, her hands over her eyes like an expectant child awaiting a surprise. Her hair curled softly on the shoulders of her pearl-gray shirt which was tucked into a pair of dark, trim-fitting slacks. She looked so good, Jack had to resist the temptation to ditch the birthday celebration in favor of more adult activities.

"What are you doing, anyway?" she asked apprehensively. "Should I be getting worried?"

"Patience, patience." He fetched the small, carefully wrapped gift he'd bought and held it for a moment, watching her. He'd imagined her here so many times, in his house, eating the food he'd cooked for her, sharing a quiet evening. Being part of his life. He wanted to savor each moment as long as he could.

He loved the way she smelled, the sound of her voice. The very sight of her caused a biological response that filled him with unbelievable contentment and certainty. He placed the gift on the mantel, then retrieved his sax from the corner and propped it against the sofa. "All right. You can open your eyes now."

Ellin laughed when she saw what he'd done, and Jack knew he had to spend the rest of his life making her happy.

"Ah, you shouldn't have." She smiled up at him.

He smiled back.

"No, I mean it, Jack. You really shouldn't have."

"What's wrong with it?" He sat down next to her and examined the wobbly, candle-covered concoction constructed out of neon pink, coconut-covered, goo-filled, snowball-shaped snack cakes. "I think it's an architectural marvel."

"I think it's a fire hazard," she said with a laugh. "I may have finally discovered something you are *not* good at." She poked the sugar-laden offering with one finger.

She started to lick off the frosting, but he caught her hand and finished the job for her. Her breath quickened at the intimacy, and her eyes widened in surprise. Jack could see his future in their whiskey-colored depths, and it took all his self-control to keep the promise he'd made earlier. He'd tough it out. He would not take advantage. But he would most certainly make himself readily available if she felt compelled to do so.

"Okay. So I'm no French pastry chef. Hold on while I play the birthday song, then blow out the candles fast before we have to call in the fire brigade."

He lifted the polished tenor sax he'd been playing since junior high, placed the reed between his lips and arrayed his fingers on the keys. He closed his eyes and finessed a slow, blues-inspired version of the popular melody, improvising a few seductive jazz notes that would have startled the original composer. When he finished, she applauded his efforts, and the candles guttered in the moving air.

"Thank you, thank you very much." It was a really bad Elvis impression, but it elicited a laugh of pleasure from her and that was what he lived for. "Go!" He waved his hands, redirecting her attention to the cake so he could hide the present behind his back.

She drew in a deep breath, then extinguished the flickering flames with a couple of strong puffs. Thin columns of smoke lingered in the air. "There. Do I get my fire safety badge now?"

"Later. Did you make a wish?" he asked softly.

"Yes, I did."

"Care to tell me what it was?"

She shook her head. "Then it wouldn't come true. Thanks for the serenade. That was an incredible rendition."

"You know what they say about sax players, don't you?"

She appeared to think for a moment. "Yes, I think I do. Old sax players never die, they just grow too pooped to pucker."

"Never. In fact, because of the workout our lips get, we actually become masterful kissers with a lot of staying power."

"I seem to recall."

He grinned as a flush of remembrance crept over her face. At least he'd made a lasting impression. "Maybe this will make up for the cake." He presented the silver-wrapped package with a flourish.

"Jack, you didn't have to—"

"Open it." He could tell she was pleased as he watched her peel the paper off the small, velvet-lined box.

"Oh, it's beautiful." She lifted out the silver heart pendant engraved with an elaborate "E," and held it by the delicate chain.

"It's a locket, look inside."

She snapped open the tiny hasp and sighed when she saw the miniature photograph of Lizzie. "Oh, it's my baby. But I don't recognize this picture. How did you—"

"Do you like it?"

"I love it. Thank you, Jack."

"I stopped by Mrs. Kendall's house one day and took a whole roll of film trying to get a shot that would work."

"I'm touched," she whispered, her voice clogged with tears. "No one's ever gone to so much trouble for my birthday before."

*No one has ever loved you like I do, Ellin. And no one ever will.* "I'm glad you like it. Here, stand up and let me put it on for you." He took the necklace and opened the catch. He held it out, and she ducked inside the circle of his arms so that he could fasten it around her neck. He breathed in the intoxicating scent of her perfume, and his body yearned toward hers. He wanted to hold her close within his embrace and never let her go. Instead he lifted her hair, laid his chin on her shoulder and pressed his lips gently to her neck.

Ellin was shaken by the powerful mix of wonder and desire that resulted from Jack's simple caress. He had touched some wellspring of need within her, and she felt its heated demand war with resolution. It would be a battle not to cross the line and become physically involved with him, and she didn't relish the struggle. This sweet, gentle man had crept into her heart. It would be so much easier, so much more honest, just to surrender to the sensations flooding through her like a drug.

She turned in his arms and rested her head against his chest. He sighed and tightened his hold on her. Then he lifted her chin and gazed into her eyes for a long moment.

"I made you a promise, and I'm a man of my word," he said. "But I really need to kiss you right now, Ellin Bennett. Would you consider it taking advantage if I did?"

She moaned because she knew she was lost. How could she maintain the necessary distance when all she wanted was to know every part of him? How could she think about the future when the moment demanded so much of her attention? "Will you please just shut up and get on with it?"

He smiled and held her face between his hands as his tongue traced the outline of her lips. She drank in the sweetness of his kiss, but when his tongue dipped inside, her body arched into his of its own volition. The kiss grew more insistent as his firm, moist mouth demanded her response.

She gave herself freely to the passion flowing between them. Her hands ached to touch him and slipped beneath his sweater to caress the length of his back. His muscles corded under her fingertips, and she felt him shudder with pleasure.

Jack kicked off his loafers and fell back on the sofa, pulling Ellin's willing body with him, their lips still melded in a slow, mind-stealing kiss. He stretched out and settled her on top of him, the full length of her curvy body pressed against his. His mouth moved over hers, devouring its lush warmth until he though he might die from the pleasure. He knew it was doing him extensive bodily damage, but he hoped it never stopped.

He had to catch his breath, so he dropped his head back

on the cushion and pulled hers down to his chest to stroke her hair. He really wanted to pace himself, to prolong the pleasure. But then she pushed up his sweater and trailed a long line of slow kisses from his stomach to his neck and back again. Pacing suddenly seemed unnecessarily prudent. He needed flesh on flesh. His fingers sought the buttons on her blouse.

She raised herself on her arms so he could work them free and part the fabric. He released the front closure of her bra, pushed the lacy garment aside and cupped the delicate weight of her breasts. The filigreed silver heart swung between them, mere inches from his face. She sighed in surrender as he massaged her silken skin until her nipples pebbled. When his tongue swept over them, she moaned out loud.

Ellin knew she was rapidly losing control of the situation. She'd had such good intentions when she promised herself not to let this happen. She'd thought to manage the matter with her head, as she'd always done in the past. She didn't expect to want his skin on hers so badly that she would rip his sweater over his head and toss it on the floor. She never bargained on being overcome by desire so profound that it burned through her like a brush fire and smoldered in that long neglected spot.

She pressed her breasts against his smooth chest and the kisses that had been gentle and searching became fiercely urgent. She yielded to them with erotic pleasure unlike any she had ever known.

Oh, she had not only crossed the line, she had obliterated it. Tomorrow would be easier if she would just end this lust-arousing exploration right now. Before it was too late. She could still preserve their friendship if things didn't go any further. Then when the time came to leave town, she could do so without all the regrets that were sure to follow the consummation of this impetuous act.

She could do that. If she weren't so needy. If it didn't feel so darned good. She knew she was shameless, but tomorrow be damned. Every fiber of her being was focused on tonight. She exalted in the clean, young beauty of him and knew she was too weak to do the right thing. She might never have an opportunity to be this fulfilled again. She couldn't throw it away. Nor could she think anymore. All the blood had drained downward from her brain to throb in an area that had no ability to be rational.

What she wanted now was to experience everything the amazing English-teaching, fire-fighting, saxophone-playing Jack Madden had to offer.

When Jack felt Ellin's hands go to the button on his jeans, he knew they were rapidly approaching the point of no return. His body was screaming like a psychotic general ordering the troops over the top and into battle, but his overdeveloped, busy mind was trying to understand what was happening here. And why. This afternoon when he decided to crank up the plan, he never dreamed they would get from birthday cake to birthday suits so quickly.

He'd dreamed of rolling around naked with Ellin Bennett for several weeks now. He was ready. He was more than willing. But he was also worried. Things were moving too fast. Where were the whispered words of love? The happily-ever-after promises? The make-like-a-swan-and-mate-for-life commitment?

If Ellin didn't need those things as much as he did, then it was too soon. They were rushing the guns. He had a future at stake here. He wasn't about to trade a lifetime of loving for a here-and-now tryst.

No matter what General Testosterone had to say.

She slipped her hand down the front of his jeans and

rubbed the evidence of his body's willingness to forego the hearts and flowers routine in favor of primate lovemaking. Damn. It was times like this he really resented having such high moral fiber. It would be so much easier, to say nothing of way more fun, if he could just take what Ellin was offering and deal with the casualties later.

But this was his life mate he was talking about here. His future wife. "The One." An important part of "The Plan" stipulated that their first time be a tender, metaphysical joining of souls, not a frenzied copulation on the couch. He wanted it to be a warm memory for Ellin to cherish always. Not a mistake she would regret in the cold light of morning. Feeling like a deserter to the cause, he groaned and captured her questing hand in his.

"Ellin? Honey? We may have missed a few steps here." His voice sounded as ragged as he felt. He hoped his words didn't sound as stupid. "As much as I hate to say this, I think we should slow things down."

Ellin didn't want to go slow. She'd paid the price to hop aboard the sexual roller coaster, and she was ready for the ride.

But evidently she had misread Jack's intentions because he had thrown on the brakes. God, what was wrong with her? She was sprawled, bare-chested, atop the most delightful man she'd ever met, and he'd just had to remove her hand from his pants. Could things get any more humiliating than this?

She tried to move away from him, but he held her fast. He reached up and dragged a velvety throw over their rapidly cooling bodies. Thank goodness, the lights were dimmed. She didn't think she could look him in the eye right now.

"I'm sorry," she said. "I didn't mean to—"

He stopped the words by kissing her deeply. "God, I hope you meant it. If you didn't, then I'm just too easy."

She moaned in dismay and covered her face with her hand. "I feel terrible."

"Really?" he asked in surprise. "Because I feel fantastic." He slipped out from under her and tucked her against his side so that when he rolled them over they could lie heart to heart. He gathered her close and caressed her arm under the throw. "I hate to think you were just toying with my affections."

"That's not what I meant," she tried to explain. "Nothing like this has ever happened before. I mean, I've had sex. I'm a mother, after all. But I never got so swept away that I couldn't think."

He smiled. "Ain't it great?"

"I have actually been called the Ice Queen. To my face. I'm always in control."

"That's not necessarily the best place to be," he pointed out.

"But I promised myself I wouldn't let this happen."

"So what changed your mind?" he asked curiously. "It was the cake, wasn't it?"

She laughed, and the embarrassment was gone. This was Jack. Man of good heart and honest words. She should have known he would make things right. "No, it was the saxophone. And the buffed-up lips. And the rippling muscles. And the, should I go on?"

"Please do."

"The locket. And the Stroganoff. And the fact that you went to so much trouble to celebrate my birthday. Thank you for stopping me before—"

"Wait a minute. I never said we had to stop." He wrapped her in his arms. "Perish the thought. I only said we should slow down and cover all the bases. I'm amenable to picking up right where we left off." He placed her hand on the front of his unzipped jeans to prove it. "But there's something I want to say first."

"No, let me." She touched her fingertips to his lips. "I was selfish. I wanted you tonight, Jack. I wanted the experience of you, even if it was just this one time. But that's not fair because in a few weeks I'll be leaving, and I know long-distance relationships simply do not work."

"It doesn't have to be that way. You don't have to leave."

"There's nothing for me to do here. I've sent out résumés and I know I can get another job. I need to support Lizzie and plan for her future. I can't do that here."

"Of course you can." Jack had to convince Ellin that her future was here, with him. He hadn't made much progress in that department during the last six weeks, but he still had six more to go. He had to smooth things over so that she wouldn't run away from him, and they could have those weeks together.

"Doing what?" she asked. "There's only one newspaper, and it already has an editor. I have to leave Washington. You could, too."

"Ellin, please don't ask me to do that."

"Then don't ask me to stay." She pushed her hair behind her shoulder. "Face it, Jack. We're too far apart on the compromise continuum. I can't stay, and you can't go. We're the ultimate example of the impossible situation. That's why I can't let myself get emotionally involved with you. I'm really sorry if I gave you the wrong idea earlier."

When he didn't respond, Ellin worried she'd said too much. That she had hurt his tender feelings, and that was something she had never intended to do. "Please say something."

"I love you, Ellin," he whispered.

She gasped at the sincerity of his declaration. And the implications. "No. That's not what you were supposed to say."

"It's true. You're 'The One' for me. I've known it since the first day we met. You're my other half, and I've been sitting here waiting for you all my life. Why else do you think you ended up in Washington, Arkansas? Do you really think fate is perverse enough to send you here just to put out twelve issues of the *Post-Ette* and leave?"

"No, no, no. Don't say that." She tried to pull away from him but he held her close. "I'm not anybody's 'One.' I've learned to accept that I'm meant to be alone. That's why my marriage failed. That's why I'm so dedicated to my job."

"*That* is the silliest piece of self-deluding rationalization I've ever heard," he told her. "I've already explained why your marriage failed. You were never meant to be with Andrew Bennett. And you're dedicated to your job because you're good at it. And you're good at it because for years you have sublimated all your sexual energy into work."

"Thank you, Dr. Freud. Is there an additional fee for the psychoanalysis? Or is it just another perk like the saxophone serenade?"

"Ellin, don't get all defensive and testy. We can work this out."

"Maybe I don't want to. Have you ever considered that maybe I'm not interested in working it out? Now where are my clothes?" She sat up and yanked the throw around her shoulders. "I need to go home. Damn! My car's not here. Where are my shoes?"

"Ellin?"

"What?"

"Calm down." Jack found her bra and shirt on the floor. She had the throw wrapped around her like a Titanic survivor and he had to tug to get it away from her. She protested, but he helped her into her clothes and buttoned her shirt. Then he fished under the couch until he found her shoes which he placed on her feet.

"There," he said. "Do you feel better now that you're fully clothed?"

"Yes, I do, thank you very much." She scurried after his sweater and held it out at arm's length. She didn't trust herself to get close enough to dress him.

"You're welcome." He slipped it on, then turned his back to zip up his jeans, before stepping into the loafers he'd kicked under the coffee table. "Now that everyone is decent again, may I finish what I was trying so incompetently to say?"

"Go ahead, but keep it brief." She sat on the edge of the couch and put her hands in her lap. "I need to go home."

Jack paced the hardwood floor in front of her, his hands fisted behind his back. "Brief it is, then. I am putting you on notice, Ellin Bennett."

"I beg your pardon?"

"A one-night stand is not acceptable to me. Neither is a two-nighter or even a forty-two nighter. You and I will not engage in wild, uninhibited sex and then go our separate ways."

"I never meant—"

"Furthermore, when we *do* engage in wild, uninhibited sex, and I hope it's soon because I can't take much more of this, it will be with the mutual understanding that we will continue doing so for the rest of our lives." He paused to let the significance of his words sink in.

"Jack, I—"

He held his hand out to shush her. "I'm sorry if I led you on, but I refuse to allow you to use me as a sexual object to gratify your depraved needs. I'm just not that kind of guy.''

Ellin was so astounded by his little speech that she could only sit and stare at him for several moments. Then she burst out laughing in appreciation of his drama skills. ''Are you finished?''

''Pretty much. However, you should be warned.''

''About what?''

''I've never been very good at taking no for an answer.''

# Chapter Eleven

"Whatever tax evasion you're in the midst of, stop right now and talk to me." Depressed by the uncharacteristically downbeat tone of his own voice, Jack slumped into the chair across from his sister's desk.

Jana looked up from the spreadsheet displayed on the monitor, shoved the computer's keyboard tray out of her way and offered him her undivided attention. "What's wrong, little brother? Bad day on cafeteria duty?"

"Worse."

"Sounds serious. How can I help?"

"Do you happen to know how to make any hillbilly love potions or voodoo charms?" he asked hopefully.

"Nope, sorry." She perked up. "I found a really good recipe for barbecue sauce on the Internet, though."

He ignored that remark, unable to appreciate her wisecracks today. "What I need is magic, but I'll settle for sisterly advice."

She placed her hands on her desk. "The doctor is in, dear brother. What's the problem?"

"It's March."

"No need to remind an accountant of the date this time of year, bub. In four weeks Tax Hell will be over, and I can have a life again."

"And in *two* weeks Ellin will leave Washington for parts unknown. That is, unless I can change her mind and convince her to stay. If I can't, *my* life will be over."

"So the uptown girl has successfully deflected the old Madden charm by activating her force field, huh?"

Jack gave her a look warning her not to try and jolly him out of it this time. He was too worried to rise to the bait of her witticisms. "I really thought we were making progress. It *felt* like progress. We talked, hung out. Shared things. We even had a little rendezvous in the laundry room. There were too many kissy-face activities going on for her not to be interested. 'The Plan' was firmly in place."

"So what happened?"

"I don't know. I had Ellin over on her birthday, which just happens to be Valentine's Day. I cooked dinner, gave her a pretty trinket, played the happy birthday song on the sax. In short, a good time was had by all."

"Sounds promising."

"But ever since that night, she's gone out of her way to avoid me. She won't talk to me or see me outside the office, not even with Lizzie along. She acts as though we've never been more than co-workers or casual acquaintances. I don't understand it. The Stroganoff wasn't *that* bad."

"Oh, no." Jana's horrified face searched his bewildered one. "You didn't. Did you? Please say you didn't."

He stared at her. "Didn't what?"

"I know you, Jack. I know how your big lumpy brain works. You didn't tell Ellin you loved her, did you?"

"Well, yeah. What's wrong with that? I've never loved any woman the way I love her."

Jana groaned. "Please say you didn't tell her about the Madden men's tradition of whirlwind courtships."

He nodded, unsure where this was leading.

"But surely, you didn't make the mating-like-swans analogy." She winced. "Did you?"

"Yeah, I think I might have. What are you getting at?"

Jana reached across the desk and smacked him on the arm. "Einstein! You can't just come right out and tell someone like Ellin Bennett that you love her. Especially not two months after you meet her."

"Why not?" Now Jack was really confused. He'd grown up with the knowledge that when the right woman came along, he would recognize her. Okay. Fate had brought this perfect love into his life, and he knew they belonged together as surely as he knew his own name. Now his sister was telling him he was supposed to keep it to himself?

"For an intelligent man, you are *so* dense. You scared her, Jack. No," Jana corrected, "you terrified her. She's probably stringing a garlic necklace right this minute to ward you off."

"Scared her? I don't understand. I'm not the threatening-male type. Hey, I'm sensitive. I'm in touch with my inner child. What's so damned frightening about me?"

"You're perfect," she told him. "That's what's scary. You are simply too good to be true."

"Now that's just mean."

"It's true." Jana smiled sadly. "Even I think so, brother, and I shared a womb with you. I knew you back when you were a skinny little geek in glasses. I've watched you grow into this unbelievably wonderful man, and sometimes you don't seem real. Even to me."

His head dropped back in frustration, and he raked both

hands through his already tousled hair. "Jeez. I never realized being a nice guy was such a handicap in the romance
department."

"Jack, let me try to explain something." Jana rolled her
chair around the desk and parked it in front of him. Then
she took both his hands and held them in her own. "You
want to know what the problem is?"

"I wouldn't be here if I didn't."

"You take yourself for granted."

"Oh, thanks for enlightening me, Sis, that definitely clar-
ifies everything. I think I'll go back to the voodoo charm."

"You're this hometown hero. You don't even think that
what you do, or who you are, is anything special. And that
is precisely what *is* so special about you."

He shook his head in exasperation. "What's that got to
do with why Ellin won't give me the time of day? I thought
I'd made it clear we belong together."

"I like Ellin," Jana said. "I didn't expect to at first, but
she kind of grows on you."

"Tell me about it." She had long since taken up permanent residence in his heart.

"I've also talked to her. About her family, her ex-
husband, her failed marriage."

"She really discussed all that? You two hardly know
each other."

"Women share the intimate details of their lives with
one another," she explained. "That's how we get ac-
quainted and make connections. Men just grunt, offer each
other a beer and call it male bonding."

Jack frowned. "I think I resent that. It's not only a gross
generalization, it's—"

"It's true. Get over it."

"Fine. Just explain where this is going."

"From what she's told me, Ellin doesn't exactly have a firm foundation of trust on which to build a relationship."

"I know," he dismissed. "But all that's in the past and the past doesn't matter."

"Well, of course the past matters, you big doofus." She hauled off and whacked him solidly on the head.

"Ow! So, what can I do about it? I know how perfect we are for each other, but how do I convince her of that? The clock is ticking here, you know."

"As hard as it may be, Jack, you have to back off. Remember when we were kids, and Tramp first wandered onto the place? He was so thin and looked so hungry, but he wouldn't come up and eat the food we put out until we went in the house."

"What's a dog got to do with anything?"

"Do you remember how you wanted to build a trap, so we could catch him and take care of him? You said you knew what was best, and it was for his own good. Do you recall what Dad told you?"

"Not exactly, Jana. I was ten."

"I do. Dad said that someone must have mistreated that dog and that's why he was so scared of us. He told us he'd been hurt, and there wasn't anything we could do to make him trust us. He would have to come to it on his own. In his own time."

"I remember," he said. "At first we stood on the porch, then each day we got a little closer to the food dish. Eventually he realized we weren't going to hurt him."

"And old Tramp turned out to be the best dog we ever had. Lived with us fifteen years."

"And the moral of Jana's little fable is…?" he asked impatiently.

"Back off, Jack. Give Ellin some space. She's been hurt, so it might take a while for her to realize what a good thing you are. You've made your feelings known. Now stand on the porch. Give her time.''

He heaved a noisy sigh. ''Like I said, time is not something I have a lot of.'' He could almost hear the clock running down.

Tick. Tick. Tick.


Ellin placed the latest edition of the *Post-Ette* in the binder. Number eleven. One more to go. Jig Baker would return soon to resume shepherding duties, and her tenure here would be over. It was funny, but when she'd first arrived in town, she assumed she would be dancing on her desk at the prospect of getting back to her real life. But things weren't so black and white anymore. And her life here felt incredibly real.

She smoothed the paper's front page before shelving the binder. The lead story this week had been the city council's vote to block the gaming company's bingo hall plans. Washington would remain unbesmirched by outside corruption a little bit longer. She smiled. Chalk up another one for Jack Madden.

At least she wouldn't have him on her conscience. She'd managed to get through the past thirty days without once being in a room alone with him, which was an amazing feat given the frequency of their contact and the persistence of his efforts.

The night she attacked him on his sofa had convinced her that she could not rely on self-control where he was concerned. Moderation in all things was supposed to be good. But moderation with Jack was not an option. She couldn't have a taste without wanting the whole banquet.

So, she'd retreated back into Ice Queen mode. She knew her aloofness hurt him. She also knew how much her recent behavior had confused him. He thought he loved her, but he was young, he would get over it and love again. At least now, she could move on, able to live with herself because she'd done the honorable thing.

Ellin's hand went to the silver locket she wore inside her blouse. She'd been surprised when he gave up so easily. Based on his cocksure belief in the fate of all things, she'd expected a protracted war of the wills. Maybe he'd finally realized she really wasn't "The One" after all. Or maybe that their differences outweighed the physical attraction. Whatever the reason, Jack had apparently given up his pursuit of her. She should be glad, but she was unbelievably saddened at the thought.

"Are you about ready to go home, El?" Deanie Sue asked as she pulled on her coat. Owen hurried to help her. He was taking her out to dinner tonight to mark the one month anniversary of their first date. Then they were planning to attend the opening night of *Raymond and Julianne* in the high school auditorium.

"I need to hang around here for a little while." She glanced at her watch. "I have an online interview with the executive editor of the *Seattle Dispatch* in an hour."

Deanie Sue gave her a hug. "I hate to think of you moving so far away. We're going to miss you, El. You really shook people up around here. You made us look at things with new eyes."

Owen returned her smile. He no longer worshipped his darling from afar. He gave Ellin's shoulder an awkward pat. "I wish you'd stay on with us, but I reckon you got bigger fish to fry."

"Something like that. You two get out of here," she told them. "Enjoy your dinner and maybe I'll see you at the play." The people of Washington had done more than make her look at things in a different light. They'd taught her to think less and feel more. It was too bad, really. Thinking wasn't nearly as painful.

Deanie Sue stopped at the door. "The wind's blowing something fierce out there. The radio said we're in for a late season storm. We don't have 'em very often, but when we do, they can be doozies, what with the ice and all. You be careful tonight, El."

"Thanks for the warning. Good night. And have fun." She straightened her desk and puttered around the office. Finally, she sat at the computer and played a few games of solitaire while she waited for her interview to begin. She already had an offer from a bigger paper in St. Louis. But Seattle was farther away. Two whole time zones from Arkansas. She could only hope the geographical and emotional distance would be enough to put Jack out of her mind.

And her heart.

An hour and a half later, the interview concluded with a firm job offer. She wouldn't make her final decision until she completed her on-site visit in a couple of weeks, but she was sure she would take it. Accepting the position of managing editor meant the achievement of a longtime goal. The *Dispatch* might not be the biggest paper in Seattle, but it had an excellent reputation, and she could advance quickly there. The salary was more than she'd expected, and the city was purported to be one of the most livable in the country.

And most importantly, moving to the Pacific Northwest would put Lizzie near Andrew. That's why she'd applied for the job, and why she would turn down the better one in St. Louis. Ellin already knew how hard it would be for her daughter to leave Washington.

Like a wildflower, she'd put down tenuous little roots and blossomed here, in the dead of an Ozark winter. She'd forged a strong relationship with her great-grandmother and gained a number of friends, among both the children and the adults of the town. She had a special attachment to one adult in particular, and Ellin knew her little girl would miss him most of all.

She hoped that by giving Lizzie an opportunity to strengthen bonds with her father, she might lessen the pain of parting. It had been slow in coming, but the last few months had taught Ellin the importance of family. It was too late for her; her father was dead, her mother busy and self-involved. But she should give Lizzie a chance to have it. Perhaps in time, Andrew would come around and make the effort to find a place for himself in his daughter's life.

Unfortunately, there was no place in her own life for Jack. She knew that now. As much as she would miss him, she no longer believed it was possible to maintain their relationship on any level. They were clearly not meant to be platonic friends. The chemistry between them was too powerful. A clean break was best for all concerned.

She called home to check on Lizzie before leaving for the play. Ida Faye had attended the afternoon student matinee because she didn't like being out late. She said everything was fine at home and for her to mind the weather and drive with care.

Ellin's mood was too glum to enjoy spending the evening watching Jack at his most charming and much-admired best, but she had no choice. He was the driving force behind the show, and it was her job to cover the event for next week's *Post-Ette*. It would be her last edition. She wanted to make it her best.

When she could find no more excuses to delay, she stepped outside and into a blast of frigid air that seemed to have blown straight down from the Arctic. She hoped the bad weather didn't damage the budding apple trees, a very important crop to the local growers. She saw that the first daffodils of the season had already bloomed in the planters along Main Street. The sudden, unseasonably cold temperature would freeze them on their stems.

Ellin started her car and waited for the engine to warm. She felt a sad kinship with those poor drooping yellow blooms. Her feelings for Jack had blossomed just as brightly, just as prematurely. And like the daffodils, her feelings could not survive cold reality.

The play went off without a hitch, earning the student performers a standing ovation from the audience. After the last curtain call, the leading lady pulled Jack center front so his troupe could thank him for his hard work and guidance. The young lady blushed through her stage makeup as she laid a bunch of long-stemmed yellow roses in his arms, along with a plaque acknowledging his part in bringing this year's production to a successful conclusion.

After the presentation, Ellin went backstage to interview the actors for the piece she would write. She was putting away her notebook when Jack approached her.

"Did you like the play?" he asked, as though all the applause, roses, and standing ovations in the world meant nothing without her approval.

"It was wonderful. Such a talented group of young people. You must be very proud of them." She pulled on her coat in preparation to leave the auditorium.

"I need to talk to you, Ellin. Could you come over to my house later? Just for a little while?"

"That probably isn't a good idea." Her cheeks reddened at the memory of what had transpired during her last visit. Just standing close to him among the scurrying stage crew and prop hands made her uncomfortably warm. How could she risk being alone with him in his cozy house with the blues playing quietly in the background?

"I just want to talk," he said. "And there's something I want to give you before you go."

She hesitated. She really should tell him about tonight's interview and job offer, as well as her plan to visit Seattle. News traveled fast in a small town, and she didn't want him to hear about it from someone else.

"All right. But just for a little while."

He looked visibly relieved when she agreed. The knowledge that she wielded so much power over this man's happiness was a weight too heavy to bear.

"Great. Give me a few minutes to finish up here and you can ride with me."

"No. I'll meet you there." She wanted her car out front this time, in case her resolution failed again, and she needed to make a quick getaway.

"In an hour then?"

"Sure."

She turned away as the young wardrobe mistress approached and asked him a question about storing the costumes. Jack only half listened to his student. He was too busy watching Ellin head for the exit. He couldn't bear to think she might be walking out of his life soon.

He hadn't been completely honest with her just now. He wanted more than just to talk with her. He'd tried his damnedest to follow Jana's suggestion. He'd backed off, given Ellin the time and space she needed to trust him. But time was running out, and he couldn't wait any longer. It was now or never.

Tonight would be the culmination of "The Plan."

Tonight Jack Madden would ask Ellin Bennett to be his wife.

As soon as he could get away, Jack hurried home through

the wind and spitting sleet. He placed the roses in a vase on the table and the bottle of champagne on ice. He lit candles he'd placed around the living room and squirted some ginger-spicy scent in the air. He fluffed the sofa pillows, and tossed the letter he'd received from Jig Baker on the coffee table. All the while he was filled with unbearable tension and excitement.

He flopped down on the couch and glanced at the clock on the mantel, then opened the jeweler's box containing the diamond solitaire he'd purchased. He would only get one shot at this, and he hoped like hell he was handling it the right way. He'd worked everything out in his mind, rehearsing answers for all her questions, reassurances for all her doubts.

Still, despite his romantic machinations, there was a strong possibility that Ellin would turn his proposal down flat. If that happened he hoped he would be man enough to let her go without making too big a fool of himself.

Maybe it was too soon to share his feelings, but he wanted to spend the rest of his life with this woman, and he wanted to start soon. He couldn't live with himself if he let this opportunity slip through his fingers. He couldn't let her leave without telling her how much he loved her.

He jumped up when the doorbell rang, nervous but excited. He stuffed the jeweler's box deep into his pocket, and prayed all the way to the door.

*Come on, Fate. Shine down on me tonight.*

# Chapter Twelve

Ellin knew she was in trouble the minute she walked into Jack's house. Candlelight bathed the living room in a warm glow. Soft Spanish guitar music played in the background. A bottle of chilled champagne stood on the coffee table, and the flowers his students gave him filled the room with the sweet scent of roses. If this was how he set the stage for a simple conversation, how would he plot a seduction?

And why was she thinking about such things?

Jack had changed from his preppy teacher's clothes into charcoal-colored wool slacks and a black turtleneck sweater. He looked so dangerously attractive that she was tempted to turn around and run for the car. Surely, everything she wanted to say could be put into an e-mail message.

He showed her in and settled beside her on the couch. "I've missed you," he said without preamble.

"I've been busy." His words set off that old alarm in her brain. *Careful, Bennett. Don't do anything stupid.*

"Actually, you've been avoiding me." He corrected her

with an easy grin. "But you're here now. That's all that matters."

"I can't stay long," she reminded him. "The weather's bad, and I should get home soon."

"Better get down to business, then." He popped open the champagne, filled two glasses and handed her one. "Help me celebrate."

"What's the occasion?"

"I finished my novel."

"Congratulations. I know you've been working on it awhile."

"Yeah, since I haven't had much social life for the past few weeks, I had a lot of time on my hands." He eased closer, his dark eyes full of challenge behind his trademark wire-rims.

She didn't trust that look. The last time he gazed at her so intently, she melted all over him. Right here, on this very couch. She slid away from him. That wasn't going to happen tonight. Her self-control was once more fully functional.

He lifted his glass. "To the future."

"Right. To the future." She touched her glass to his and sipped the sparkling wine. "And to your publishing success."

"I did it for the process. Emotional catharsis and all that. I don't really care if it gets published."

"That's about the dumbest thing I ever heard." She set her glass down. "Why work so hard and put so much time and energy into a project if you're not going to reap the reward?"

"Work is its own reward." He clucked his tongue. "I thought you would have learned that by now. 'There is only one success—to be able to spend your life in your own way.'"

"Says who?"

"Well, that was a quote from Christopher Morley. But I tend to agree with him."

"Still, you should send your manuscript out. I can give you the names of some people."

"I'll keep that in mind." He reached for the airmail envelope on the table and opened it as though he'd already lost interest in his own work. "I got this letter from Jig Baker yesterday. He says he's enjoying his sabbatical so much he's thinking of retiring so he can pursue archaeology full-time."

"Really? I thought that was just a hobby."

"It was, but the university extended the dig, and his friend is willing to let him continue assisting the team, in a kind of a learn-as-you-go capacity."

"What about the *Post-Ette?*" The little paper might not be much in the great journalism scheme of things, but it served a valuable purpose in the community. She'd invested three months in it, and would hate to see it fold.

"Funny you should ask," he said with a big smile. "Jig wants to sell it. He wrote to see if I knew anyone who might be interested. You could buy yourself a newspaper on the cheap. Just make the man an offer he can't refuse."

The suggestion took her by surprise. "I don't have that kind of money."

"Go see Paul Davis over at First Farmers' Bank. I've spoken to him already, and he's willing to help you close the deal."

"You talked to people about this?"

"I was just testing the water," he said.

"Well, you shouldn't have troubled yourself. I'm not going to buy the *Post-Ette*. I only agreed to come here tonight because I have something to tell you, and I didn't want you to hear it through the grapevine."

"What's that?"

As he leaned toward her, his arm slid along the back of the sofa in a casual embrace. She felt her self-control slowly dissolving in the heat of his nearness. Too late, she realized that coming here had been a fatal mistake.

"I've had some online interviews," she blurted before she could act on the impulses clamoring for action. "In fact, I had one with the head of the *Seattle Dispatch* today. He offered me the position of managing editor."

He didn't say anything for several moments. When he spoke his voice was strained and tight. "That's what you've always wanted, isn't it?"

"I plan to fly up there soon and check it out. I've made up my mind." She didn't tell him about the offer in St. Louis. Doing so would serve no useful purpose. "If I like the city, I'll take the job."

Jack's confidence drained away, replaced with cold doubt. For the first time, he realized he might actually lose Ellin. And Lizzie. He thrust his hand into his pocket and touched the jeweler's box like a talisman. The ring it contained belonged on her finger. He had to make his move now, before it was too late.

"Ellin, I—"

"I've thought it out," she interrupted before he could ask the most important question of his life. "I'm doing this for Lizzie."

"Lizzie likes it here," he reminded her.

"Maybe. But she needs to be near her father. I can't keep her from him the way my mother kept me from my dad. I regret not knowing him better, and I resent my mother keeping us apart."

She told him about the cards her grandmother had given her and how they had filled her with remorse. "My ex-husband may not be the most involved parent, but he's Lizzie's father, and she needs to spend time with him."

She thought of the job in St. Louis. It promised more money. More prestige. More career points. But she couldn't take it. "A few months ago, the daddy problem never would have influenced my decision. I would have done whatever advanced my career. But living here, knowing you, I've learned the importance of family. I have to give Lizzie and Andrew a chance."

Jack sighed and raked his fingers through his hair. He'd read enough literature to recognize irony when it punched him in the gut. He'd spent the last three months showing Ellin that the bonds of family and friends were more important than individual success or achievement. He'd taught her well, it seemed, because she had learned the lesson and was using it to buy a one-way ticket out of his life.

He'd been so wrapped up in thoughts of a future with Ellin that he hadn't factored Lizzie's needs into the equation. Fathering her had set easy in his mind. He'd wrongly assumed that the three of them would make their own family.

The little girl adored him, and he adored her back. But that wasn't enough. Lizzie already had a father. Jack's grip on the ring box tightened, as though he could squeeze a solution to this dilemma from it.

"Maybe I could move there, too," he suggested with a casualness that belied his growing sense of dread. "I'm a good teacher. I could find a job."

"No, Jack. It wouldn't work. You belong here. People depend on you." Ellin felt the hot sting of tears and panicked. She never cried and couldn't afford to start now. She needed to be strong to get through this. Tears would only make her vulnerable.

"I don't need anyone but you."

"That's the sweetest lie I ever heard. You're the heart of this town. You wouldn't be happy anywhere else. This is your home."

"It could be yours, too."

"I can't stay."

"But if we give up now, we'll never know what we could have had together."

"I'm no good at relationships. You deserve someone who can return all the love you give."

"You're saying you could never love me?"

No, she couldn't say that. But a clean break was best. She ached at the thought of living without him, and her only solace was knowing she was doing the right thing.

"I'm saying I *can't* love you, Jack. I'm taking Lizzie to Seattle so she won't grow up without a father. You find yourself a nice girl. One with no obligations or shadows in her past. Marry her. Have your own child. Live a long and happy life."

"But you're 'The One' for me. I love you and Lizzie. I want you two to be my family."

"You'll find someone. A man like you will never be alone for long." She stood up before he could stop her, and took her coat from the closet.

Jack squeezed the box again as his frantic thoughts sought a solution. When he received the letter from Jig, he'd hoped Ellin would jump at the chance to run her own newspaper, even if it was an eight-page country weekly. He'd been sure the career obstacle was the biggest problem they had to overcome. His hopeful heart had deceived him into thinking he could win her love.

But this? He hadn't seen it coming. What he hadn't bargained for, and what he simply couldn't do, was keep the little girl he'd grown to love from her father. He selfishly wanted to be the most important man in both their lives, but he knew with an awful certainty that he had to let them go.

Ellin stood with one hand on the door knob. "Oh. You said earlier you wanted to give me something. Were you talking about your manuscript?"

"Yeah," he said softly. "That's what I was talking about." It was the hardest thing he ever had to do, but Jack pushed the jeweler's box deep into his pocket and slowly withdrew his hand. He stepped into his study, quickly composed himself and returned with a flat manuscript box.

"I'll read it as soon as I can."

"No hurry."

"I'm honored you want me to read it. I'll be happy to give you whatever editorial comments I can."

Editorial comments? That was the last thing in the world he wanted from Ellin Bennett. "Good night."

"Goodbye, Jack." She hurried down the steps and dashed through the cold drizzle to her car.

He stood on the porch, watched until she backed out of the drive and disappeared into the night.

"But I don't want to move," Lizzie cried the next day when she overheard Ellin telling Ida Faye her plans over Saturday morning coffee.

"But Seattle is a nice place. You can visit the ocean, feed the seagulls."

"I don't want to visit the ocean." She clamped both small fists on nonexistent hips. "And I hate nasty old seagulls. I want to stay with Grammy in Washton."

Ellin pulled her daughter into her lap. "Remember, honey, Daddy lives in Seattle. You'll be able to see him more often."

Lizzie's lower lip protruded in a classic pout. "I don't care. I want to stay here." She jumped down and ran to her room, still dressed in her bright red footie pajamas. Ellin flinched when she heard the eloquent slam of the door.

"Leave the child be," Ida Faye said when she started after her. "Give her time to cool off. You can't reason with a four-year-old no how. You'd just be wasting your breath."

Ellin hugged her grandmother whose recovery from hip surgery was now complete. "You understand why I'm leaving, don't you?"

"I understand," she grumbled. "Don't mean I have to like it."

Ellin smiled. They had already discussed the move and her plans for securing their newly made bonds. "Thanks, Grammy. I'll be in my room finishing some reading I started last night. Call me when you're ready for me to make lunch."

Three hours later, she laid Jack's manuscript beside her on the bed. Moved to tears by the story and the insight it gave her into Jack's life, she opened the drawer in the bedside table to search for a tissue. When she removed the box, she saw the packet of cards beneath it.

She'd left them there to remind her of missed opportunities. And she'd used them to justify her decision to take Lizzie to Seattle. But reading Jack's novel had made her wonder if running away meant she was missing the greatest opportunity of all.

*The Shape of Home* recounted the experiences of a journalism student interning in a strife-torn eastern African nation. A young man's idealism shattered by the inhumanity he witnesses. The senseless slaughter and the decimated villages. The innocents made to suffer for racial identity. Starving children, children armed with guns, and those with limbs blown off by land mines. Though trained to be objective, he cannot simply report injustice. He must fight it.

Disillusioned, he closes the door between his spirit and the world. He retreats to his safe Midwestern hometown where children aren't murdered for ethnic reasons that no longer have meaning. He becomes a teacher because he believes his only hope to change the world is to touch the future, one child at a time.

Ellin picked up the manuscript and clasped it to her chest. Without a doubt, the novel was autobiographical. Jack had poured his soul onto the pages. She knew that like the young protagonist, he had experienced the effects of guerrilla warfare firsthand. It was the only way he could have written about such heartbreaking events so vividly.

And yet, he'd been unwilling to talk about it, even when she had asked him outright. But that didn't surprise her. Jack's strength did not lie in imposing his views but rather in leading others to understanding through the example he set. She'd been a fool to think he was wasting his talent in Washington, Arkansas. All the time she'd thought he wasn't doing enough, he was doing what most men could only aspire to. Living his beliefs.

She turned again to the final page of his manuscript and read aloud the passage in which the protagonist explains his choices by quoting Ralph Waldo Emerson. "To laugh often and much; to win the respect of intelligent people and the affection of children…to leave the world a better place…to know even one life has breathed easier because you lived. This is to have succeeded."

"Ellin? Is Lizzie in here with you?" Ida Faye poked her head in the room. "I fell asleep in my chair, and when I woke up I couldn't find her."

"Isn't she in her room?"

"I thought she was, but I've looked all over, and I can't find her anyplace."

"She's just upset about the move. She's probably hiding

somewhere.'' Ellin dashed through the small house, searching every room, under beds and behind furniture. When it became clear she was not in the house, a cold knot of fear formed in her stomach.

''Ellin!''

The panic in her grandmother's voice turned Ellin's blood to ice. She ran into the kitchen and as soon as she saw the older woman's pale face, she knew something was terribly wrong.

''The laundry room door was open.'' When Ida Faye reached for her hat and coat on the peg nearby she noticed Lizzie's purple snowsuit hanging there. ''She's gone outside without her wrap. We have to find her, it's freezing out there.''

''I'll go after her,'' Ellin said. She couldn't risk having her grandmother fall again. ''You stay here in case she comes back. Call 911 and report her missing. The more people we have looking, the sooner we'll find her.''

Ellin thrust her arms into her own jacket and pulled the hood over her head. She stepped outside and a gust of wind filled with icy sleet struck her in the face.

Jack was lying on the couch, twirling the ring Ellin would never wear around and around on his little finger. He debated whether or not to return it to the store. He'd just about decided to keep it as an expensive reminder of dreams too foolish to come true. He was startled when the call came through on his first responder radio. He stuck the ring back in its box as he listened to the dispatcher. When he heard Lizzie was lost, he absently stuffed the box in his pocket, ran to his pickup and headed for the house on Dogwood Street.

Ellin was in a panic when he got there. She'd scoured the neighborhood, but no one had seen the little girl in the red fleece pajamas. He hugged her close and reassured her they would find Lizzie. When another responder showed up, Jack left him to organize the others and took Ellin to look for her missing child.

Half the town turned out to search. The local Boy Scouts canvassed the neighborhoods door to door. Lizzie's sitter, Mrs. Kendall commandeered concerned housewives through downtown businesses. Hal Madden and his fire-fighters organized volunteers who searched the town in grids.

"Try not to worry, Ellin." Jack hoped to ease the dis-traught mother's mind, but his own was troubled when the search net had to be extended to outlying areas. "We'll find her."

"But it's so cold, and she's so little. She's only wearing pajamas. We have to find her before it gets dark."

Jack hugged her, and knew from the way she trembled in his arms that she was close to falling apart. "I said we'd find her, Ellin, and we will."

"What if she's been kidnapped? God, if anything hap-pens to her, I'll never forgive myself."

"This is Washington," he reminded her. "She hasn't been kidnapped. She just wandered off. She'll be fine." But doubt began to plague him as another frustrating hour went by.

Lizzie Bennett had been missing nearly five hours. Be-cause of the weather, it was nearly dark when Jack turned his truck down a little-used road on the edge of town.

He saw the worried question in Ellin's eyes. "There's an old barn down here. The owner uses it to store hay and grain. Let's take a look around before we head back."

She leaned heavily against him on the seat. He reached over and squeezed her hand reassuringly, but he didn't like to think about Lizzie being out alone in the dark. He parked near the barn and switched on the portable searchlight.

"Lizzie! Baby, are you in here?" His words echoed in the still evening air. He fanned the light around the barn's dark interior, and his heart jumped when he spotted a swatch of red in the hay manger in the corner. "Lizzie!"

"Oh, thank God, it's her." Ellin went weak with relief when she saw her precious child sit up in the straw and knuckle the sleep from her eyes.

When Lizzie recognized her rescuers, she scrambled to her feet and ran toward them. She rushed past her mother and hurled herself straight into Jack's outstretched arms.

"Oh, Jack. I got losted." She wrapped her tiny arms tightly around his neck.

"What happened, honey?" He was so damned glad to hold her, safe and almost warm from her nap in the hay. "Everybody's been looking for you." He removed his coat and wrapped it around her.

"I saw a kitty outside. I wanted to catch it so it wouldn't be cold. But it runned away, and I chased it, and then I got losted. But I was waiting for you. I knowed you would find me, Jack. I'm glad you comed." She buried her face against his neck.

"I'm glad I found you, too, baby." He hugged her close, knowing he might hold her for the moment, but too soon, he would lose this child of his heart forever. Along with the only woman he had ever loved.

He cleared the emotion from his voice, got on the radio and called off the search. When he was done, he held the radio up to Lizzie's mouth. "Tell everyone you're all right."

"I'm all right," she yelled into it. "My Jack finded me.

"There's my kitty," she squealed as a young cat stretched and yawned its way out of the straw. "Can I keep him?"

"I think you'll have to." Jack scooped up the ball of

gray fur and tucked it inside his coat with her. "Ready to go home?"

"Will you go with me?"

"Of course I will." He kissed her cheek.

Ellin's heart had almost stopped when her daughter sought comfort in Jack's arms instead of her own. Her relief at finding Lizzie safe was soon overwhelmed by guilt. Had she been so preoccupied with providing for her child that she'd failed to give her the nurturing she needed? Had her daughter learned, at the ripe old age of four, not to count on her mother for the important things? No career was worth losing that trust.

Jack held Lizzie and gazed at Ellin over her blond head. Everything he couldn't say, was in his eyes. "I love you, Ellin. I can't bear to lose you and Lizzie. Don't leave me."

"I love you too, Jack." The words surprised her, but the conviction they gave her was the most exhilarating feeling she had ever known. She didn't have to do it all herself. And she didn't have to go through life alone.

She couldn't let another perfect chance slip away. Not when he stood before her with so much love in his eyes.

"Here, honey." Jack reached in his pocket, pulled out the velvet box and handed it to Lizzie, including her in his proposal. "Show this to Mommy. Ask her if she'll wear it for me."

Lizzie's little fingers fumbled with the lid. She opened it and gasped when she saw the sparkling diamond inside. "Jack got you this pretty ring, Mommy. You want it, don't you?"

"Yes, I want it. Very much." Ellin smiled through tears of joy. She didn't have to move halfway across the country to give her daughter a family. Why hadn't she realized it before? Biology did not make a father. Love did. Jack was the dependable rock Lizzie would turn to again and again as she grew up. She was already more important to him than she would ever be to the self-centered man whose genes she carried.

Holding Lizzie safe in his arms, Jack pulled off Ellin's glove with his teeth. He lifted the ring from the box, took her trembling hand in his own shaky one and slipped it onto her finger.

She loved him even more when she realized he must have planned to give it to her the night before. He'd kept quiet when she announced she was leaving for Lizzie's sake. That realization convinced her that she was right to bind her life to his.

Why had it taken her so long to recognize what had been right in front of her all along? This tender teacher had taught her life's most important lesson.

"It fits," she said.

"I never doubted it." He kissed her, deeply and sweetly while the child they would rear together looked on. "I plan to spend the rest of my life making you and Lizzie happy."

And Ellin knew he would do it. Because Jack Madden was a man who kept his promises.

\* \* \* \* \*

SILHOUETTE *Romance*™

**Lost siblings, secret worlds,
tender seduction—live the fantasy in...**

A TALE OF THE SEA

**Separated and hidden since childhood,
Phoebe, Kai, Saegar and Thalassa
must reunite in order to safeguard
their underwater kingdom.
But who will protect *them*...?**

***Look for these titles wherever
Silhouette books are sold!***

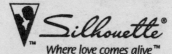

*Where love comes alive*™

Visit Silhouette at www.eHarlequin.com          SRTOS

**Where royalty and romance
go hand in hand...**

The series continues in Silhouette Romance
with these unforgettable novels:

**HER ROYAL HUSBAND**
by Cara Colter
on sale July 2002 (SR #1600)

**THE PRINCESS HAS AMNESIA!**
by Patricia Thayer
on sale August 2002 (SR #1606)

**SEARCHING FOR HER PRINCE**
by Karen Rose Smith
on sale September 2002 (SR #1612)

And look for more Crown and Glory stories in
SILHOUETTE DESIRE starting in October 2002!

*Available at your favorite retail outlet.*

*Where love comes alive™*

**You've shared love, tears and laughter.**

**Now share your love of reading—**

**give your daughter Silhouette Romance® novels.**

**Where Texas society reigns supreme—and appearances are *everything*.**

**Coming in June 2002**
*Stroke of Fortune* **by Christine Rimmer**

Millionaire rancher and eligible bachelor Flynt Carson struck a hole in one when his Sunday golf ritual at the Lone Star Country Club unveiled an abandoned baby girl. Flynt felt he had no business raising a child, and desperately needed the help of former flame Josie Lavender. Though this woman was too innocent for his tarnished soul, the love-struck nanny was determined to help him raise the mysterious baby—and what happened next was anyone's guess!

*Available at your favorite retail outlet.*

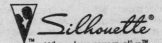

If you enjoyed what you just read,
then we've got an offer you can't resist!

# Take 2 bestselling
# love stories FREE!

# Plus get a FREE surprise gift!

# COMING NEXT MONTH

**#1600 HER ROYAL HUSBAND—Cara Colter**
*Crown and Glory*
Prince Owen had once known love with beautiful American
Jordan Ashbury. Back then, she'd fallen for the man, not the royal
title he'd kept secret. But when she came to work in the palace
kitchen five years later—her young daughter in tow—he found he
wasn't the only one who'd kept a secret....

**#1601 MARRIED IN THE MORNING—Susan Meier**
Waking up in Gerrick Green's Vegas hotel room was embarrassing
enough for Gina Martin, until she saw the wedding ring on her finger. She'd married the enemy—the man bent on taking over her
father's company. But would love prove stronger than ambition?

**#1602 MORE THAN MEETS THE EYE—Carla Cassidy**
*A Tale of the Sea*
Investigator Kevin Cartwright was assigned to track down four siblings separated during childhood. Seeing Dr. Phoebe Jones on TV
wasn't the break he'd been expecting, nor was falling for the shy,
attractive scholar with a strange fear of the sea. But would the
shocking mysteries of her past stand between them?

**#1603 PREGNANT AND PROTECTED—Lilian Darcy**
Being trapped beneath a collapsed building bonded newly pregnant
Lauren Van Schulyer and a handsome stranger called Lock. Six
months later, the mom-to-be met the man her father hired to protect
her—Daniel "Lock" Lachlan! The single dad guarded Lauren's
body, but he was the only one who could steal her heart....

**#1604 LET'S PRETEND...—Gail Martin**
Derek Randolph needed a pretend girlfriend—fast!—to be in the
running for a promotion, so he enlisted the help of his sister's best
friend, sophisticated Jess Cossette. But would the invented romance
turn into the real thing for two former high school enemies?

**#1605 THE BRAIN & THE BEAUTY—Betsy Eliot**
Single mom Abby Melrose's young son was a genius, so who
else could Abby turn to for help but a former child prodigy? Yet
embittered Jeremy Waters only wanted to be left alone. Did the
beauty dare to tame the sexy, reclusive beast—and open his heart
to love?